CHRISTOPHER

The

Watsons

GO TO

BIRMINGHAM

1963

25TH-ANNIVERSARY EDITION

A YEARLING BOOK

Text copyright © 1995 by Christopher Paul Curtis
Foreword and afterword copyright © 2020 by Christopher Paul Curtis
Tribute by Kate DiCamillo copyright © 2020 by Kate DiCamillo
Tribute by Varian Johnson copyright © 2020 by Varian Johnson
Tribute by Jacqueline Woodson copyright © 2020 by Jacqueline Woodson
Map copyright © 2020 by Charity Ekpo
Cover art copyright © 2020 by Katrina Damkoehler

Visit us on the Web! rhcbooks.com

Educators and librarians, for a variety of teaching tools, visit us at RHTeachersLibrarians.com

Library of Congress Cataloging-in-Publication Data is available upon request.
ISBN 978-0-593-30649-9 (pbk.)

Printed in the United States of America

10 9 8 7 6 5 4 3 2 1

Yearling Anniversary Edition 2020

Also by
CHRISTOPHER PAUL CURTIS

The Mighty Miss Malone

Mr. Chickee's Messy Mission

Mr. Chickee's Funny Money

Bucking the Sarge

Bud, Not Buddy

This book is dedicated to my parents,
Dr. Herman and Leslie Lewis Curtis,
who have given their children both
roots and wings and encouraged us to soar;
and to my sister, Cydney Eleanor Curtis,
who has been unfailingly supportive,
kind and herself.

In memory of

Addie Mae Collins
Born 4/18/49, died 9/15/63

Denise McNair
Born 11/17/51, died 9/15/63

Carole Robertson
Born 4/24/49, died 9/15/63

Cynthia Wesley
Born 4/30/49, died 9/15/63

the toll for one day in one city

FOREWORD
Christoper Paul Curtis

The Watsons Go to Birmingham—1963 saved my life.

It was 1993, I was forty years old and my life was at a crossroad. I had quit a spirit-crushing, thirteen-year-long job at Flint's Fisher Body car factory and spent seven years in limbo, bouncing from one dead-end temporary staffing agency job to the next. I'd come to picture my life as a huge ocean liner churning its way along at differing speeds, sometimes chugging mightily, but more frequently mired in the doldrums. I even gave the ship a name: the SS *Christopher.*

As a child, living in my parents' home, I sat comfortably on the deck of this ship, never considering that the kindness, warmth, and love I was experiencing were neither promised nor eternal.

Sometime around 1966, thirteen-year-old Christopher was strolling the decks of that ship and was smacked in the mouth by unexpected turbulence. I'm not sure what hit me, but I found myself washed overboard, buffeted in the ship's wake as it left me behind.

I went from a cheerful, "academically talented," well-adjusted thirteen-year-old who was vice president of the student council to a sullen thirteen-year-old whose one career aspiration was to become a hermit.

Was adolescence the tsunami that swept me overboard, or was it the gut punch of watching my old neighborhood being ground to ashes and dust for something called "urban renewal"? Maybe it was the trauma of going from an all-Black elementary school and neighborhood to a new junior high and neighborhood that were 98 percent white.

There's an old Canadian joke about the vast, flat emptiness of the Manitoba prairies. The gist is that a Winnipeg man's girlfriend left him and he sat on his front porch for three weeks watching as she walked away.

That's how I felt as I spent decades watching the SS *Christopher* shrink into the horizon. Occasionally I'd be inspired to start stroking to try to catch it, but most of the time, I'd tread water and think, what's the point?

In my early forties I had a temp job at a warehouse unloading trucks in Allen Park, Michigan. After one particularly rough day, the words of my dear old friend Alvin Stockard came back to me: "You'll never get a hit if you don't at least swing the bat."

I decided to have one more go at catching that receding ship.

I'd always suspected I could write a book. For the next year I dedicated nearly every day to sitting in the Windsor Public Library working on a novel about a Flint family's trip "down home." The result was the manuscript for *The Watsons Go to Birmingham—1963*. When I finished I entered two contests for beginning novelists: I submitted my novel to Delacorte Press and to another publisher, and went back to the tedium of unloading trucks and waiting.

It didn't take long for the second publishing house to turn the book down with a personalized rejection letter, which every writing magazine I'd read said is a real accomplishment and cause for pride.

But, man, after the editor wrote that "While your characters seem real and funny and overall your story is good, I'm afraid it simply will not resonate with young readers after the final page is turned," I felt as though I had been hugged from head to toe by a straight razor! I realized if Delacorte's First Contemporary Young Adult Fiction Contest turned me down, that would be the end of my nonexistent writing career.

I've never understood Herman Melville–like writers who are strong enough to expose themselves to scores of rejection letters. If two separate people from major publishing houses told me something wasn't good, I could see no benefit in having that judgment confirmed by thirty or forty other editors.

There are no lessons to be learned from the second kick of a mule.

Salvation, however, can come from the oddest of places.

A life ring splashed in front of me one afternoon when I got home from the warehouse to find a message on my answering machine. A bubbly, enthusiastic woman had left a message telling me *The Watsons Go to Birmingham—1963* was "too young" to win the Delacorte contest, but she added, "We like it so much we're going to publish it anyway!"

She promised I'd be hearing from her soon. She said her name was Wendy Lamb.

Wendy Lamb? Really? Wendy Lamb? "Wendy Lamb" sounded like the perfect name some lame, low-creativity prankster would give to a children's book editor.

But Wendy Lamb turned out to be largely legit, and

after our first conversation I let out a long-held sigh.

To my surprise and joy, I looked down and found my dripping feet back on the deck of the SS *Christopher*.

The Watsons Go to Birmingham—1963 saved my life. And now it's celebrating its twenty-fifth anniversary.

And what an appropriate time for this to be happening!

Not so long ago, I had become more and more pessimistic about the human condition and our country's future. The late sixties were turbulent times, but I've always felt those years were a halcyon period of American history. An era most nobly represented by the Freedom Riders, a group of courageous young African American and white people who literally put their lives on the line for the civil rights of all Americans. I'd come to believe that the brief moment in time when a multiracial, multireligious group of young people came together to work for change was ephemeral and long gone.

I'd seen almost no evidence of that spirit since.

Imagine my surprise and joy as I watched news reports of the resurgence of that spirit through the Black Lives Matter movement. As I witnessed an army of young African American, white, Latinx, and Asian faces in the streets of cities across the United States, Canada, and the world, demanding justice. All triggered improbably by the horrific and tragic killing of one Black man, George Floyd.

It does look as though the times they are a-changing.

These selfless young activists have provided a defibrillating shock to my spirits. When I think of how many of them were born after *The Watsons* was first published, and realize that there's a good possibility some teacher may have introduced one of them to Kenny, Byron, and Joetta, I am even more joyful. I'm moved to tears when I think that even one of these brave young people may have taken to heart the words I wrote twenty-five years ago in this book's epilogue: "These freedom fighters are the true American heroes. They are the boys and girls, the women and men who have seen that things are wrong and have not been afraid to ask 'Why can't we change this?' They are the people who believe that as long as one person is being treated unfairly, we all are. These are our heroes, and they still walk among us today. One of them may be sitting next to you as you read this, or standing in the next room making your dinner, or waiting for you to come outside and play.

"One of them may be you."

June 2020

The Watsons

GO TO

BIRMINGHAM

1963

1. And You Wonder Why We Get Called the Weird Watsons

I t was one of those super-duper-cold Saturdays. One of those days that when you breathed out your breath kind of hung frozen in the air like a hunk of smoke and you could walk along and look exactly like a train blowing out big, fat, white puffs of smoke.

It was so cold that if you were stupid enough to go outside your eyes would automatically blink a thousand times all by themselves, probably so the juice inside of them wouldn't freeze up. It was so cold that if you spit, the slob would be an ice cube before it hit the ground. It was about a zillion degrees below zero.

It was even cold inside our house. We put sweaters and hats and scarves and three pairs of socks on and still were cold. The thermostat was turned all the way up and the furnace was banging and sounding like it was about to blow up but it still felt like Jack Frost had moved in with us.

All of my family sat real close together on the couch under a blanket. Dad said this would generate a little heat but he didn't have to tell us this, it seemed like the cold automatically made us want to get together and huddle up. My little sister, Joetta, sat in the middle and all you could see were her eyes because she had a scarf wrapped around her head. I was next to her, and on the outside was my mother.

Momma was the only one who wasn't born in Flint so the cold was coldest to her. All you could see were her eyes too, and they were shooting bad looks at Dad. She always blamed him for bringing her all the way from Alabama to Michigan, a state she called a giant icebox. Dad was bundled up on the other side of Joey, trying to look at anything but Momma. Next to Dad, sitting with a little space between them, was my older brother, Byron.

Byron had just turned thirteen so he was officially a teenage juvenile delinquent and didn't think it was "cool" to touch anybody or let anyone touch him, even if it meant he froze to death. Byron had tucked the blanket between him and Dad down into the cushion of the couch to make sure he couldn't be touched.

Dad turned on the TV to try to make us forget how cold we were but all that did was get him in trouble. There was a special news report on Channel 12 telling about how bad the weather was and Dad groaned when the guy said, "If you think it's cold now, wait until tonight, the temperature is expected to drop into record-low territory, possibly reaching the negative twenties! In fact, we won't be seeing anything above zero for the next four to five days!" He was smiling when he said this but none of the Watson family thought it was funny. We all looked over at Dad. He just shook his head and pulled the blanket over his eyes.

Then the guy on TV said, "Here's a little something we can use to brighten our spirits and give us some hope for the future: The temperature in Atlanta, Georgia, is forecast to reach . . ." Dad coughed real loud and jumped off the couch to turn the TV off but we all heard the weatherman say, ". . . the mid-seventies!" The guy might as well have tied Dad to a tree and said, "Ready, aim, fire!"

"Atlanta!" Momma said. "That's a hundred and fifty miles from home!"

"Wilona . . . ," Dad said.

"I knew it," Momma said. "I knew I should have listened to Moses Henderson!"

"Who?" I asked.

Dad said, "Oh Lord, not that sorry story. You've got to let me tell about what happened with him."

Momma said, "There's not a whole lot to tell, just a story about a young girl who made a bad choice. But if you do tell it, make sure you get all the facts right."

We all huddled as close as we could get because we knew Dad was going to try to make us forget about being cold by cutting up. Me and Joey started smiling right away, and Byron tried to look cool and bored.

"Kids," Dad said, "I almost wasn't your father. You guys came real close to having a clown for a daddy named Hambone Henderson. . . ."

"Daniel Watson, you stop right there. You're the one

who started that 'Hambone' nonsense. Before you started that everyone called him his Christian name, Moses. And he was a respectable boy too, he wasn't a clown at all."

"But the name stuck, didn't it? Hambone Henderson. Me and your granddaddy called him that because the boy had a head shaped just like a hambone, had more knots and bumps on his head than a dinosaur. So as you guys sit here giving me these dirty looks because it's a little chilly outside ask yourselves if you'd rather be a little cool or go through life being known as the Hambonettes."

Me and Joey cracked up, Byron kind of chuckled and Momma put her hand over her mouth. She did this whenever she was going to give a smile because she had a great big gap between her front teeth. If Momma thought something was funny, first you'd see her trying to keep her lips together to hide the gap, then, if the smile got to be too strong, you'd see the gap for a hot second before Momma's hand would come up to cover it, then she'd crack up too.

Laughing only encouraged Dad to cut up more, so when he saw the whole family thinking he was funny he really started putting on a show.

He stood in front of the TV. "Yup, Hambone Henderson proposed to your mother around the same time I did. Fought dirty too, told your momma a pack of lies about me and when she didn't believe them he told her a pack of lies about Flint."

Dad started talking Southern-style, imitating this

4

Hambone guy. "Wilona, I heard tell about the weather up that far north in Flint, Mitch-again, heard it's colder than inside a icebox. Seen a movie about it, think it was made in Flint. Movie called *Nanook of the North*. Yup, do believe for sure it was made in Flint. Uh-huh, Flint, Mitch-again.

"Folks there live in these things called igloos. According to what I seen in this here movie most the folks in Flint is Chinese. Don't believe I seen nan one colored person in the whole dang city. You a 'Bama gal, don't believe you'd be too happy living in no igloo. Ain't got nothing against 'em, but don't believe you'd be too happy living 'mongst a whole slew of Chinese folks. Don't believe you'd like the food. Only thing them Chinese folks in that movie et was whales and seals. Don't believe you'd like no whale meat. Don't taste a lick like chicken. Don't taste like pork at all."

Momma pulled her hand away from her mouth. "Daniel Watson, you are one lying man! Only thing you said that was true was that being in Flint is like living in a igloo. I knew I should have listened to Moses. Maybe these babies mighta been born with lumpy heads but at least they'da had *warm* lumpy heads!

"You know Birmingham is a good place, and I don't mean just the weather either. The life is slower, the people are friendlier—"

"Oh yeah," Dad interrupted, "they're a laugh a minute down there. Let's see, where was that 'Coloreds Only' bathroom downtown?"

"Daniel, you know what I mean, things aren't perfect

but people are more honest about the way they feel"—
she took her mean eyes off Dad and put them on
Byron—"and folks there do know how to respect their
parents."

Byron rolled his eyes like he didn't care. All he did
was tuck the blanket farther into the couch's cushion.

Dad didn't like the direction the conversation was
going so he called the landlord for the hundredth time.
The phone was still busy.

"That snake in the grass has got his phone off the
hook. Well, it's going to be too cold to stay here tonight, let me call Cydney. She just had that new furnace
put in, maybe we can spend the night there." Aunt
Cydney was kind of mean but her house was always
warm so we kept our fingers crossed that she was home.

Everyone, even Byron, cheered when Dad got Aunt
Cydney and she told us to hurry over before we froze to
death.

Dad went out to try and get the Brown Bomber
started. That was what we called our car. It was a 1948
Plymouth that was dull brown and real big, Byron said it
was turd brown. Uncle Bud gave it to Dad when it was
thirteen years old and we'd had it for two years. Me and
Dad took real good care of it but some of the time it
didn't like to start up in the winter.

After five minutes Dad came back in huffing and
puffing and slapping his arms across his chest.

"Well, it was touch and go for a while, but the Great
Brown One pulled through again!" Everyone cheered,

but me and Byron quit cheering and started frowning right away. By the way Dad smiled at us we knew what was coming next. Dad pulled two ice scrapers out of his pocket and said, "O.K., boys, let's get out there and knock those windows out."

We moaned and groaned and put some more coats on and went outside to scrape the car's windows. I could tell by the way he was pouting that Byron was going to try and get out of doing his share of the work.

"I'm not going to do your part, Byron, you'd better do it and I'm not playing either."

"Shut up, punk."

I went over to the Brown Bomber's passenger side and started hacking away at the scab of ice that was all over the windows. I finished Momma's window and took a break. Scraping ice off of windows when it's that cold can kill you!

I didn't hear any sound coming from the other side of the car so I yelled out, "I'm serious, Byron, I'm not doing that side too, and I'm only going to do half the windshield, I don't care what you do to me." The windshield on the Bomber wasn't like the new 1963 cars, it had a big bar running down the middle of it, dividing it in half.

"Shut your stupid mouth, I got something more important to do right now."

I peeked around the back of the car to see what By was up to. The only thing he'd scraped off was the outside mirror and he was bending down to look at himself in it. He saw me and said, "You know what, square? I must be adopted, there just ain't no way two folks as ugly as your momma and daddy coulda give birth to someone as sharp as me!"

He was running his hands over his head like he was brushing his hair.

I said, "Forget you," and went back over to the other side of the car to finish the back window. I had half of the ice off when I had to stop again and catch my breath. I heard Byron mumble my name.

I said, "You think I'm stupid? It's not going to work this time." He mumbled my name again. It sounded like his mouth was full of something. I knew this was a trick, I knew this was going to be How to Survive a Blizzard, Part Two.

How to Survive a Blizzard, Part One had been last night when I was outside playing in the snow and Byron and his running buddy, Buphead, came walking by. Buphead has officially been a juvenile delinquent even longer than Byron.

"Say, kid," By had said, "you wanna learn somethin' that might save your stupid life one day?"

I should have known better, but I was bored and I think maybe the cold weather was making my brain slow, so I said, "What's that?"

"We gonna teach you how to survive a blizzard."

"How?"

Byron put his hands in front of his face and said, "This is the most important thing to remember, O.K.?"

"Why?"

"Well, first we gotta show you what it feels like to be trapped in a blizzard. You ready?" He whispered something to Buphead and they both laughed.

"I'm ready."

I should have known that the only reason Buphead and By would want to play with me was to do something mean.

"O.K.," By said, "first thing you gotta worry about is high winds."

Byron and Buphead each grabbed one of my arms and one of my legs and swung me between them going, "*Wooo*, blizzard warnings! Blizzard warnings! *Wooo*! Take cover!"

Buphead counted to three and on the third swing they let me go in the air. I landed headfirst in a snowbank.

But that was O.K. because I had on three coats, two sweaters, a T-shirt, three pairs of pants and four socks along with a scarf, a hat and a hood. These guys couldn't have hurt me if they'd thrown me off the Empire State Building!

After I climbed out of the snowbank they started laughing and so did I.

"Cool, Baby Bruh," By said, "you passed that part of the test with a B-plus, what you think, Buphead?"

Buphead said, "Yeah, I'd give the little punk a A."

They whispered some more and started laughing again.

"O.K.," By said, "second thing you gotta learn is how to keep your balance in a high wind. You gotta be good at this so you don't get blowed into no polar bear dens."

They put me in between them and started making me spin round and round, it seemed like they spun me for about half an hour. When slob started flying out of my mouth they let me stop and I wobbled around for a while before they pushed me back in the same snowbank.

When everything stopped going in circles I got up and we all laughed again.

They whispered some more and then By said, "What you think, Buphead? He kept his balance a good long time, I'm gonna give him a A-minus."

"I ain't as hard a grader as you, I'ma give the little punk a double A-minus."

"O.K., Kenny, now the last part of Surviving a Blizzard, you ready?"

"Yup!"

"You passed the wind test and did real good on the balance test but now we gotta see if you ready to graduate. You remember what we told you was the most important part about survivin'?"

"Yup!"

"O.K., here we go. Buphead, tell him 'bout the final exam."

Buphead turned me around to look at him, putting my back to Byron. "O.K., square," he started, "I wanna make sure you ready for this one, you done so good so far I wanna make sure you don't blow it at graduation time. You think you ready?"

I nodded, getting ready to be thrown in the snowbank real hard this time. I made up my mind I wasn't going to cry or anything, I made up my mind that no matter how hard they threw me in that snow I was going to get up laughing.

"O.K.," Buphead said, "everything's cool, you 'member what your brother said about puttin' your hands up?"

"Like this?" I covered my face with my gloves.

"Yeah, that's it!" Buphead looked over my shoulder at Byron and then said, "*Wooo*! High winds, blowing snow! *Wooo*! Look out! Blizzard a-comin'! Death around the corner! Look out!"

Byron mumbled my name and I turned around to see why his voice sounded so funny. As soon as I looked at him Byron blasted me in the face with a mouthful of snow.

Man! It was hard to believe how much stuff By could put in his mouth! Him and Buphead just about died laughing as I stood there with snow and spit and ice dripping off of my face.

Byron caught his breath and said, "Aww, man, you flunked! You done so good, then you go and flunk the Blowin' Snow section of How to Survive a Blizzard, you forgot to put your hands up! What you say, Buphead, F?"

"Yeah, double F-minus!"

It was a good thing my face was numb from the cold

already or I might have froze to death. I was too embarrassed about getting tricked to tell on them so I went in the house and watched TV.

So as me and By scraped the ice off the Brown Bomber I wasn't going to get fooled again. I kept on chopping ice off the back window and ignored By's mumbling voice.

The next time I took a little rest Byron was still calling my name but sounding like he had something in his mouth. He was saying, "Keh-ee! Keh-ee! Hel' . . . hel' . . . !" When he started banging on the door of the car I went to take a peek at what was going on.

By was leaned over the outside mirror, looking at something in it real close. Big puffs of steam were coming out of the side of the mirror.

I picked up a big, hard chunk of ice to get ready for Byron's trick.

"Keh-ee! Keh-ee! Hel' me! Hel' me! Go geh Momma! Go geh Mom-ma! Huwwy uh!"

"I'm not playing, Byron! I'm not that stupid! You'd better start doing your side of the car or I'll tear you up with this iceball."

He banged his hand against the car harder and started stomping his feet. "Oh, please, Keh-ee! Hel' me, go geh Mom-ma!"

I raised the ice chunk over my head. "I'm not playing, By, you better get busy or I'm telling Dad."

I moved closer and when I got right next to him I could see boogers running out of his nose and tears running down his cheeks. These weren't tears from the cold either, these were big juicy crybaby tears! I dropped my ice chunk.

"By! What's wrong?"

"Hel' me! Keh-ee! Go geh hel'!"

I moved closer. I couldn't believe my eyes! Byron's mouth was frozen on the mirror! He was as stuck as a fly on flypaper!

I could have done a lot of stuff to him. If it had been me with my lips stuck on something like this he'd have tortured me for a couple of days before he got help. Not me, though, I nearly broke my neck trying to get into the house to rescue Byron.

As soon as I ran through the front door Momma, Dad and Joey all yelled, "Close that door!"

"Momma, quick! It's By! He's froze up outside!"

No one seemed too impressed.

I screamed, "Really! He's froze to the car! Help! He's crying!"

That shook them up. You could cut Byron's head off and he probably wouldn't cry.

"Kenneth Bernard Watson, what on earth are you talking about?"

"Momma, please hurry up!"

Momma, Dad and Joey threw on some extra coats and followed me to the Brown Bomber.

The fly was still stuck and buzzing. "Oh, Mom-ma! Hel' me! Geh me offa 'ere!"

"Oh my Lord!" Momma screamed, and I thought

she was going to do one of those movie-style faints, she even put her hand over her forehead and staggered back a little bit.

Joey, of course, started crying right along with Byron.

Dad was doing his best not to explode laughing. Big puffs of smoke were coming out of his nose and mouth as he tried to squeeze his laughs down. Finally he put his head on his arms and leaned against the car's hood and howled.

"Byron," Momma said, gently wiping tears off his cheeks with the end of her scarf, "it's O.K., sweetheart, how'd this happen?" She sounded like she was going to be crying in a minute herself.

Dad raised his head and said, "Why are you asking how it happened? Can't you tell, Wilona? This little knucklehead was kissing his reflection in the mirror and got his lips stuck!" Dad took a real deep breath. "Is your tongue stuck too?"

"No! Quit teasin', Da-ee! Hel'! Hel'!"

"Well, at least the boy hadn't gotten too passionate with himself!" Dad thought that was hilarious and put his head back on his arms.

Momma didn't see anything funny. "Daniel Watson! What are we gonna do? What do y'all do when this happens up he-uh?" Momma started talking Southern-style when she got worried. Instead of saying "here" she said "he-uh" and instead of saying "you all" she said "y'all."

Dad stopped laughing long enough to say, "Wilona,

14

I've lived in Flint all my life, thirty-five years, and I swear this is the first time I've ever seen anyone with their lips frozen to a mirror. Honey, I don't know what to do, wait till he thaws out?"

"Pull him off, Dad," I suggested. Byron went nuts! He started banging his hands on the Brown Bomber's doors again and mumbling, "No! No! Mom-ma, doe leh him!"

Joey blubbered out, "This is just like that horrible story Kenny read me about that guy Nar-sissy who stared at himself so long he forgot to eat and starved to death. Mommy, please save him!" She went over and hugged her arms around stupid Byron's waist.

Momma asked Dad, "What about hot water? Couldn't we pour enough hot water on the mirror so it would warm up and he could get off?" She kept wiping tears off By's cheeks and said, "Don't you worry, Baby, we gonna get you off of this." But her voice was so shaky and Southern that I wondered if we'd be driving around in the summer with a skeleton dangling from the outside mirror by its lips.

Dad said, "I don't know, pouring water on him might be the worst thing to do, but it might be our only chance. Why don't you go get some hot tap water and I'll stay to wipe his cheeks."

Joey told By, "Don't worry, we'll come right back." She stood on her tiptoes and gave By a kiss, then she and Momma ran inside. Dad cracked up all over again.

"Well, lover boy, I guess this means no one can call you Hot Lips, can they?"

Dad was killing himself. "Or the Last of the Red Hot Lovers either, huh?" He tugged on Byron's ear a little, pulling his face back.

By went nuts again. "Doe do dat! Mom-ma! Mom-ma, hel'! Keh-ee, go geh Mom-ma! Huwwy!"

"Hmm, I guess that's not going to work, is it?"

Every time he wiped away the tears and the little mustache of boogers on Byron's lip Dad couldn't help laughing, until a little river of tears was coming out of his eyes too.

Dad tried to straighten his face out when Momma and Joey came running back with a steaming glass of hot water, but the tears were still running down his cheeks.

Momma tried to pour water on the mirror but her hands were shaking so much, she was splashing it all over the place. Dad tried too, but he couldn't look at Byron without laughing and shaking.

That meant I had to do it.

I knew that if my lips were frozen on something and everybody was shaking too much to pour water on them except for Byron he'd do some real cruel stuff to me. He probably would have "accidentally" splashed my eyes until they were frozen open or put water in my ears until I couldn't hear anything, but not me. I gently poured a little stream of water over the mirror.

Dad was right! This was the worst thing we could do! The water made a cracking sound and froze solid as soon as it touched the mirror and By's lips!

Maybe By's mouth was frozen but his hands sure

weren't and he popped me right in the forehead. Hard! I hate to say it but I started crying too.

It's no wonder the neighbors called us the Weird Watsons behind our backs. There we were, all five of us standing around a car with the temperature about a million degrees below zero and each and every one of us crying!

"'top! 'top!" By yelled.

"Daniel Watson, what're we gonna do?" Momma went nuts. "You gotta get this boy to the hospital! My baby is gonna die!"

Dad tried to look serious real quick.

"Wilona, how far do you think I'd get driving down the street with this little clown attached to the mirror? What am I supposed to do, have him run beside the car all the way down to the emergency room?"

Momma looked real close at By's mouth, closed her eyes for a second like she was praying and finally said, "Daniel, you get in there and call the hospital and see what they say we should do. Joey and Kenny, go with your daddy."

Dad and Joey went crying into the house. I stayed by the Brown Bomber. I figured Momma was clearing everybody out for something. Byron did too and looked at Momma in a real nervous way.

Momma put her scarf around Byron's face and said, "Sweetheart, you know we gotta do something. I'ma try to warm your face up a little. Just relax."

"O.K., Mom-ma."

"You know I love you and wouldn't do anything to

hurt you, right?" If Momma was trying to make Byron relax she wasn't doing a real good job at it. All this talk about love and not getting hurt was making him real nervous.

"Wah are you gonna do? Huh? Doe hur' me! Keh-ee, hel'!"

Momma moved the scarf away and put one hand on Byron's chin and the other one on his forehead.

"No! Hel'! Hel' me, Keh-ee!"

Momma gave Byron's head a good hard snatch and my eyes automatically shut and my hands automatically flew up to cover my ears and my mouth automatically flew open and screamed out, "Yeeeowwww!"

I didn't see it, but I bet Byron's lips stretched a mile before they finally let go of that mirror. I bet his lips looked like a giant rubber band before they snapped away from that glass!

I didn't hear it, but I bet Byron's lips made a sound like a giant piece of paper being ripped in half!

When I opened my eyes Byron was running to the house with his hands over his mouth and Momma following right behind him. I ran over to the mirror to see how much of Byron's mouth was still stuck there.

The dirty dogs let Byron get away with not doing his share of the windows and I had to do the whole car myself. When we were finally going to Aunt Cydney's house I decided to pay Byron back for punching me in the forehead and getting out of doing his part of the window scraping. Joey was sitting between us so I felt kind of safe. I said to her, loud, "Joetta, guess what. I'm thinking about writing my own comic book."

"What about?"

"Well, it's going to be about this real mean criminal who has a terrible accident that turns him into a superhero."

Joey knew I was going to tease Byron so she sat there looking like I should be careful what I said. Finally I asked her, "Do you want to know what I'm going to call this new superhero?"

"What?"

"I'm going to call him the Lipless Wonder. All he does is beat up superheroes smaller than him and the only thing he's afraid of is a cold mirror!"

All the Weird Watsons except Byron cracked up. Momma's hand even covered her mouth. I was the only one who saw Byron flip me a dirty finger sign and try to whisper without smearing all the Vaseline Momma had put on his lips, "You wait, I'm gonna kick your little behind." Then he made his eyes go crossed, which was his favorite way of teasing me, but I didn't care, I knew who had won this time!

2. Give My Regards
to Clark, Poindexter

Larry Dunn was the king of the kindergarten to fourth grade where I went to school at Clark Elementary. He was king because he was a lot older than anyone else and twice as strong as the rest of us. He was stronger because he was almost full grown and he'd flunked some grade two or three times.

He was the third-oldest kid at Clark. The only ones older than him and stronger than him were Byron and Buphead, who were in the sixth grade and who'd also flunked some grade at least once, we weren't sure because it was something that Momma and Dad didn't talk about.

Larry Dunn was king of the kindergarten to fourth grade only because Byron didn't care about them. Larry was the king of Clark . . . but Byron was a god.

It seemed like that would make me a prince or a real strong angel or something but it didn't work that way, I was just another fourth-grade punk. I guess having the school's god as my brother did give me some kind of special rights but not a whole bunch. It helped me with stupid stuff like the time I found a dollar bill and got too excited and was crazy enough to show it to Larry Dunn. I knew this was a big mistake about a second before he stuck his hand out and said, "Lemme see it." What could I do?

"Kenny," he said, "where you find this buck?"

"Outside the school, over by Kennelworth."

Larry turned my dollar over and over, and I started getting nervous.

"You know what, Kenny?"

"What?" I held my breath.

"This is some real strange stuff but I lost fifty cents over on Kennelworth yesterday and I bet my fifty cents got hooked up with someone else's fifty cents and made this here buck."

Whew! I let my breath go, smiled and nodded. We went to the store to get change and Larry Dunn got back the fifty cents he lost and I got to keep the other fifty that got hooked up with Larry's. I knew if it wasn't for Byron being my big brother Larry would have said something like "Since my fifty cents found this other fifty cents and they hooked up to make this here buck I'm gonna keep the whole thing. You know the rules, finders keepers, losers weepers."

Having the school's god as my relative helped in some other ways too. I had two things wrong with me that would have gotten me beat up and teased a lot more than I did if it hadn't been for By. The first thing was, because I loved to read, people thought I was real smart, teachers especially.

Teachers started treating me different than other kids when I was in the first grade. At first I thought it was cool for them to think I was smart but then I found out it made me enemies with some of the other kids.

Back when I was in the second grade, Miss Henry used to take me to different classrooms and have me read stuff out of the Bible or the newspaper in front of other kids. This was a lot of fun until I started looking up from what I was reading and noticed that while Miss Henry and the other teachers were smiling a mile a minute, all the kids had their faces twisted up or were looking at me like I was a six-legged dog.

Two years ago Miss Henry took me to Mr. Alums's fifth-grade class. Mr. Alums was the toughest teacher in the school and just being in front of him was kind of scary. He looked down at me and said, "Good morning, Mr. Watson, I hope you are in good form today." I just nodded at him because I wasn't sure what that meant.

"Don't be nervous, Kenny," Miss Henry said. "Mr. Alums would like you to read a few passages from Langston Hughes." She handed me a book and said, "You wait here while we introduce you to the class."

Man! Some of the time I wished I was as smart as these teachers thought I was because if I had been I would have dropped that book and run all the way home. If I'd been smart enough to figure out what was going to happen next I would have never gone into that room.

I stood in the hall looking at the stuff they wanted me to read while Mr. Alums told his class, "All right, I have a special treat for you today. I've often told you that as Negroes the world is many times a hostile place for us." I saw Mr. Alums walking back and forth whacking a yardstick in his hand. "I've pointed out time and time again how vital it is that one be able to read well. I've stressed on numerous occasions the importance of being familiar and comfortable with literature. Today Miss Henry and I would like to give you a demonstration of your own possibilities in this regard. I want you to carefully note how advanced this second-grade student is, and I particularly want you to be aware of the effect his skills have upon you. With work you too will be capable of reading at a miraculous level."

I saw Mr. Alums point the yardstick at someone somewhere in the class and say, "Perhaps you'd like to finish the introduction, I think you know our guest quite well."

Whoever he pointed at said, "What? I didn't do nothin'."

Miss Henry waved for me to come in and stand in front of the class. I guess I was too nervous about Mr. Alums to have recognized the voice before, but as soon as I walked into the room I froze. There in the two seats closest to the teacher's desk in the very first row sat Buphead and Byron! The Langston Hughes book jumped from my hand and the whole class laughed, everyone but Byron. His eyes locked on mine and I felt things start melting inside of me.

Mr. Alums slammed the yardstick on his desk and the class got real, real quiet.

"Let's see if you find this so humorous after you've heard how well this young man reads. And Byron Watson, if you are incapable of taking some of the fire out of your eyes I assure you I will find a way to assist you.

"If, instead of trying to intimidate your young brother, you would emulate him and use that mind of yours, perhaps you'd find things much easier. Perhaps you wouldn't be making another appearance in the fifth grade next year, now would you, hmmm?" Byron got one more dirty look in at me, then looked down at his desk.

Mr. Alums might as well have tied me up to a pole and said, "Ready, aim, fire!"

I read through the Langston Hughes stuff real quick but that was a mistake. Miss Henry said, "Slow down some, Kenneth," and then she took the book from me and handed it back upside down. She had a great big smile when she told Mr. Alums, "When he goes too fast, this slows him down a bit." I read some more with the book upside down and got some real strange looks from the fifth-graders.

Finally they let me quit. Mr. Alums stood up and clapped his hands and a couple of the old kids did too. Byron never looked at me the whole time but Buphead was giving me enough dirty looks for both of them.

"Bravo! Outstanding, Mr. Watson! Your future is un-limited! Bravo!" All I could do was try to figure out how to get home alive.

I didn't even get out of the school yard before Byron and Buphead caught up to me. A little crowd bunched up around us, and everyone was real excited because they knew I was about to get jacked up.

Buphead said, "Here that little egghead punk is."

"Leave the little clown alone," Byron said. "It's a crying shame, takin' him around like a circus freak."

He punched me kind of soft in the arm and said, "At least you oughta make 'em pay you for doin' that mess. If it was me they'd be comin' out they pockets with some foldin' money every time they took me around."

I couldn't believe it. I think Byron was proud of me!

When everybody saw Byron wasn't going to do any-thing to me for being smart they all decided that they better not do anything either. I still got called Egghead or Poindexter or Professor some of the time but that wasn't bad compared to what could have happened.

The other thing that people would have teased me a lot more about if it hadn't been for Byron was my eye.

Momma said it wasn't important, that I was a real handsome little boy, but ever since I'd been born one of my eyeballs had been kind of lazy. That means instead of looking where I tell it to look, it wanted to rest in the corner of my eye next to my nose. I'd done lots of things to make it better, but none of them worked. I'd done exercises where I had to look that way, then this way, this way, then that way, up and down, down and up, but when I went to look in the mirror the eye still went back to its corner. I'd worn a patch on my other eye to make the lazy one work but that didn't do anything either. It was fun to play like I was a pirate for a while but that got boring.

Finally Byron gave me some good advice. He noticed that when I talked to people I squinched my lazy eye kind of shut or that I'd put my hand on my face to cover it. I only did this 'cause it got hard to talk to someone when they were staring at your eye instead of listening to what you had to say.

"Look, man," he told me, "if you don't want people to look at your messed-up eye you just gotta do this." Byron made me stand still and look straight ahead, then he stood on my side and told me to look at him. I turned my head to look. "Naw, man, keep your head straight and look at me sideways."

I did it. "See? You ain't cockeyed no more, your eyes is straight as a arrow now!" I went to the bathroom, stood on the toilet and leaned over to look in the mirror sideways, and Byron was right! I couldn't help smiling. Momma was right too, I was a kind of handsome little guy when I looked at myself sideways and both eyes were pointing in the same direction!

Even though my older brother was Clark Elementary School's god that didn't mean I never got teased or beat up at all. I still had to fight a lot and still got called Cockeye Kenny and I still had people stare at my eye and I still had to watch when they made their eyes go crossed when they were teasing me. It seemed like one of these things happened to me every day, but if it hadn't been for Byron I knew they'd have happened a whole lot more. That's why I was kind of nervous about what was going to happen if Byron ever got out of sixth grade and went to junior high school before I caught up to him. That's why I was going to send off for that book *Learn Karate in Three Weeks* that was in the back of my comic books.

The worst part about being teased was riding the school bus on those mornings when Byron and Buphead decided they were going to skip school.

We'd be standing on the corner waiting for the bus, Byron, Buphead and all the other old thugs in one bunch, Larry Dunn, Banky and all the other young thugs in another bunch, the regular kids like Joetta in a third bunch and me off to the side by myself. When we saw the bus about three blocks away we all got in a line—old thugs, young thugs, regular kids, then me. It wasn't until the bus stopped and the door opened that I knew whether By and Buphead were going. I hated it when By walked past and said, "Give my regards to Clark, Poindexter." Some of the time those words were like a signal for the other kids to jump on me.

But the day I stopped hating the bus so much began with those same words. We were all lined up. "Give my regards to Clark, Poindexter," By said, and disappeared around the bus's back. I got on the bus and took the seat right behind the driver. The days By rode I would sit a few rows from him in the back, on other days the driver was the most protection.

The bus drove down into public housing and after everyone was picked up we headed toward Clark. But today the bus driver did something he'd never done before. He noticed two kids running up late . . . and he stopped to let them get on. Every other time someone was late he'd just laugh at them and tell the rest of us, "This is the only way you little punks is gonna learn to be punctual. I hope that fool has a pleasant walk to school." Then no matter how hard the late kid banged on the side of the bus the driver would just take off, laughing out of the window.

That was part one of my miracle, that let me know something special was going to happen. As soon as the doors of the bus swung open and two strange new boys got on, part two of my miracle happened.

Every once in a while, Momma would make me go to Sunday school with Joey. Even though it was just a bunch of singing and coloring in coloring books and listening to Mrs. Davidson, I had learned one thing. I learned about getting saved. I learned how someone could come to you when you were feeling real, real bad and could take all of your problems away and make you feel better. I learned that the person who saved you, your personal saver, was sent by God to protect you and to help you out.

When the bigger one of the two boys who got on the bus late said to the driver in a real down-South accent,

"Thank you for stopping, sir," I knew right away. I knew that God had finally gotten sick of me being teased and picked on all the time.

As I looked at this new boy with the great big smile and the jacket with holes in the sleeves and the raggedy tennis shoes and the tore-up blue jeans I knew who he was. Maybe he didn't live a million years ago and maybe he didn't have a beard and long hair and maybe he wasn't born under a star but I knew anyway, I knew God had finally sent me some help, I knew God had finally sent me my personal saver!

As soon as the boy thanked the driver in that real polite, real country way I jerked around in my seat to see what the other kids were going to do to him. Whenever someone new started coming to Clark most of the kids took some time to see what he was like. The boys would see if he was tough or weak, if he was cool or a square, and the girls would look to see if he was cute or ugly. Then they decided how to treat him.

I knew they weren't going to waste any time with this new guy, it was going to be real easy and real quick with him. He was like nobody we'd seen before. He was raggedy, he was country, he was skinny and he was smiling at everybody a mile a minute. The boy with him had to be his little brother, he looked like a shrunk-up version of the big one.

Everyone had stopped what they were doing and were real quiet. Some were standing up to get a better look. The older one got an even bigger smile on his face and waved real hard at everybody, the little shrunk-up version of him smiled and did the same thing. Then they said, "Hiya, y'all!" and I knew that here was someone who was going to be easier for the kids to make fun of than me!

Most of the kids were just staring. Then Larry Dunn said, "Lord today, look at the nappy-headed, down-home, country corn flake the cat done drugged up from Mississippi, y'all!" About a million fingers pointed at the new kids and a million laughs almost knocked them over.

Larry Dunn threw an apple core from the back of the bus and the new kid got his hand up just in time to block it from hitting him in the face. Little bits of apple exploded all over the kid, his brother and me. The other kids went wild laughing and saying to each other, "Hiya, y'all!"

The bus driver jumped out of his seat and stood between the new kid and Larry Dunn.

"You see? You see how you kids is? This boy shows some manners and some respect and y'all want to attack him, that's why nan one of y'all's ever gonna be nothin'!" The bus driver was really mad. "Larry Dunn, you better sit your tail down and cut this mess out. I know you don't want to start panning on folks, do you? Not with what I know 'bout your momma."

Someone said, "Ooh!" and Larry sat down. The bus was real quiet. We'd never seen the driver get this mad before. He pushed the two new kids into the same seat as me and told them, "Don't you pay no mind to them little fools, they ain't happy lest they draggin' someone down." Then he had to add, "Y'all just sit next to Poindexter, he don't bother no one."

I sat there and looked at them sideways. I didn't say anything to them and they didn't say anything to me. But I was kind of surprised that God would send a saver to me in such raggedy clothes.

3 The World's Greatest
Dinosaur War Ever

I couldn't believe it! The door opened in the middle of math class and the principal pushed the older raggedy kid in. Mrs. Cordell said, "Boys and girls, we have a new student in our class starting today, his name is Rufus Fry. Now I know all of you will help make Rufus feel welcome, won't you?"

Someone sniggled.

"Good. Rufus, say hello to your new classmates, please."

He didn't smile or wave or anything, he just looked down and said real quiet, "Hi."

A couple of girls thought he was cute because they said, "Hi, Rufus."

"Why don't you sit next to Kenny and he can help you catch up with what we're doing," Mrs. Cordell said.

I couldn't believe it! I'd wanted my personal saver to be as far away from me as he could get. I knew when you had two people who were going to get teased a lot and they were close together people didn't choose one of them to tease, they picked on both of them, and instead of picking on them the normal amount they picked on them twice as much.

Mrs. Cordell pushed the new kid over to the empty seat next to me.

"Kenny, show Rufus where we are in the book."

I watched the new kid sideways. He said, "Kenny? I thought they said your name was Poindexter." The class cracked up, part from his country style of talking and part from laughing at me. I could tell that even Mrs. Cordell was fighting not to break out laughing.

Though he was looking friendly when he said this I kind of knew it had to be teasing, because whoever heard of anybody's momma giving them a name like Poindexter? When he sat down next to me I tried to imitate Byron's "Death Stare" but it didn't work because the kid smiled at me real big and said, "My name's Rufus, what are we doing?"

"Times tables."

"That's easy! You need some help?"

"No!" I said, and scooted around in my chair so all he could do was look at my back. This guy was real desperate for a friend because even though I wouldn't say much back to him he kept jabbering away at me all through class.

When lunchtime came he followed me outside right to the part of the playground where I sit to eat. He forgot about bringing a lunch so I gave him one of Momma's throat-choking peanut butter sandwiches and let him eat the last half of my apple. He really was a strange kid; he only ate half the sandwich and folded the rest up in the waxed paper and when I handed him the apple he even ate the spots where you could see my teeth had been, he didn't even wipe the slob off first.

And, man, this kid could really talk! He was yakking a mile a minute, saying stuff like "Your momma sure can make a good peanut butter sandwich" and "How come these kids is so darn mean?"

Then he said something that made me get all funny and nervous inside, he said, "How come your eyes ain't lookin' in the same way?" I looked to see if maybe this was the start of some teasing but he looked like he really wanted to know. He wasn't staring at me either, he was kind of looking down and kicking at the dirt with his raggedy shoes.

"It's a lazy eye."

He stopped kicking dirt and said, "Don't it hurt?"

"No."

He said, "Oh," then kicked a little more dirt and hollered out, "Ooh, boy! Look at how fat that there is!"

"What?"

"You don't see that squirrel?" he asked me, and pointed up at a tree across the street. "That sure is one fat, dumb squirrel!"

I looked at the squirrel, it didn't look fat or dumb to me, it was a regular old squirrel sitting on a branch chewing on something. "How come you think it's dumb?"

"What kind of squirrel sits out in the open like that with folks all round him? That squirrel wouldn't last two seconds in Arkansas, I'da picked him off easy as nothing." The new kid pointed at the squirrel like his finger was a gun and said, "Bang! Squirrel stew tonight!"

"You mean you shot a gun before?"

"Ain't you?"

"You mean you really ate a squirrel before?"

"You ain't?"

"A real, real gun?"

"Just a twenty-two."

"How's a squirrel taste?"

"It taste real good!"

"You mean you really shoot 'em with real bullets and then you really eat 'em?"

"Why else shoot 'em?"

"Real squirrels, like that one?"

"Not that fat and not that stupid. I guess all the fat, stupid ones been got already. Since I been born all that's left in Arkansas is skinny, sneaky ones. I think them Michigan squirrels is worth two Arkansas ones."

"You aren't lying?"

He raised his hand and said, "I swear for God. Ask Cody."

"Who?"

The little shrunk-up version of the new kid was

standing by himself up against the fence that runs around Clark, watching us. The new kid waved at him and his little brother came running over.

The big one pointed over at the squirrel. "Cody, lookit there!"

Cody laughed and said, "Ooh boy! That sure is a fat squirrel!"

"Think you could pick him off from here?"

Cody pointed his finger like it was a gun and said, "Bang! Squirrel stew tonight!"

I couldn't believe this little kid had shot a gun too. "You shot a real gun?"

"Just a twenty-two."

"With real bullets?"

The little one looked at his big brother to see why I was asking all this stuff. It seemed like they were trying to be patient with me, like I was a real dummy or something. The older one said, "Tell him."

"Yeah, it was real bullets, what else you gonna shoot out a gun?"

I still didn't believe them but the bell rang and lunch was over. I know he didn't think I noticed, but the big kid gave his little brother the other half of my sandwich. I guess both of them had forgot about lunch.

This saver stuff wasn't going anything like I thought it was supposed to. Rufus started acting like I was his friend. In the morning on the bus he'd always come sit next to me, and Mrs. Cordell put his regular seat next to mine in school. Every day at lunchtime he followed me out to the playground and ate half of my second sand-wich, then sneaked the other half to Cody. He even found out where we lived and started coming over every night around five-thirty.

I didn't mind him coming over to play, because both our favorite game was playing with the little plastic di-nosaurs that I had and you couldn't really have any fun playing by yourself. That was because someone had to be the American dinosaurs and someone had to be the Nazi ones. Rufus didn't even mind being the Nazi di-nosaurs most of the time and it was O.K. playing with him because he didn't cheat and didn't try to steal my plastic monsters.

The only other guy I used to play with was LJ Jones, but I quit playing with him when a lot of my dinosaurs started disappearing. I've got about a million of them but before LJ started coming over I had two million. It's kind of embarrassing how LJ got them from me. At first he'd steal them one or two at a time and I asked Byron what I should do to stop him.

By said, "Don't sweat it, punk. The way I figure it one or two of them stupid little monsters ain't a real high price for you to pay to get someone to play with you."

But LJ wasn't satisfied with doing one or two, I guess he wanted a raise, so one day he said to me, "You know, we should stop having these little fights all the time. We need to have one great big battle!"

"Yeah, we could call it the World's Greatest Dinosaur War Ever," I said, "but I get to be the Americans."

I should have known something was fishy when LJ said, "O.K., but I get first shot." Most of the time it always took a big fight to decide who had to be the Nazis.

I started setting up my dinosaurs and LJ said, "This ain't right. If this really is the World's Greatest Dinosaur War Ever we need more monsters. You should go get the rest of 'em."

He was right. If this was going to be a famous battle we needed more fighters. "O.K., I'll be right back," I said.

This wasn't going to be easy. I wasn't allowed to take all of my dinosaurs out at once because Momma was afraid I'd lose most of them. Especially because she didn't trust LJ. Every time he'd come over she'd tell me, "You watch out for that boy, he's a little too sneaky for my tastes." I had a plan, though. I'd go upstairs and drop the pillowcase I kept my dinosaurs in out of the window. I wasn't so stupid that I'd drop them down to LJ, I'd drop them out of the other side of the house and then run around to get them.

My plan worked perfect! After I went and picked up the pillowcase I set up my dinosaurs and LJ set up the Nazis and we started the battle.

He took first shot and killed about thirty of mine with an atomic bomb. My dinosaurs shot back and got twenty of his with a hand grenade. The battle was going great! Dinosaurs were falling right, left and center. We had a great big pile of dead dinosaurs off to the side and had to keep shaking more and more reinforcements out of the pillowcase. Then in the middle of one big fight LJ said, "Wait a minute, Kenny, there's something we forgot about."

I was ready for a trick. I knew LJ was going to try to get me to go away for a minute so he could steal a bunch of my monsters. I said, "What?"

"These dinosaurs been droppin' atom bombs on each other. Think about how dangerous that is."

"How's it dangerous?"

LJ said, "Look." He made one of his brontosauruses run by the pile of dead dinosaurs and when it got two steps past them it started shaking and twitching and fell over on its side, dead as a donut. LJ flipped him on the dead dinosaur pile.

I said, "What happened to him?"

"It was the radioactiveness. We gotta bury the dead ones before they infect the rest of the live ones."

Maybe it was because we had such a great war going on and I was kind of nervous about who'd win, but this stupid stuff made sense, so instead of digging each one of the couple hundred dead dinosaurs a grave we dug one giant hole and buried all the radioactive ones in it, then we put a big rock on top so no radioactivity could leak out.

This really was the World's Greatest Dinosaur War Ever. We fought and killed dinosaurs for such a long time that we had to make two more graves with two more big rocks on top of them. LJ finally pulled the trick I knew he was going to but he did it so cool that I didn't even see it coming.

"Kenny, you ever been over in Banky and Larry Dunn's fort?"

LJ knew I hadn't. "Uh-uh."

"I found out where it is."

"Where?"

"You wanna come see it?"

"Are you crazy?"

"They ain't there, this is Thursday night, they're up at the community center playin' ball."

"Really?"

"Well, if you too scared . . ."

I knew this was a worm with a hook in it but I bit anyway. "I'm not scared if you aren't."

"Let's go!"

I figured the trick would come in right here so I kept a real good eye on LJ while we put my monsters back in the pillowcase. When we were done I sneaked a look at his back pockets, 'cause I knew when he stole dinosaurs he put them back there or in his socks. From the way his pockets were sticking out it looked like he had one *Tyrannosaurus rex* and one triceratops. I couldn't tell how many he had in his socks. I figured that wasn't too bad a price for as much fun as we'd had.

LJ was talking a mile a minute. "They even got some books with nekkid ladies! You ever seen a nekkid lady?"

"Yeah, lots of times!" I had too. Byron had borrowed lots of nasty magazines from Buphead's library. I knew LJ didn't believe me, though. For some reason if you were famous for being smart no one thought you'd ever looked at a dirty book.

40

LJ said, "You gotta be in the house by seven, don't you?"

"Yeah."

"O.K., we better hurry before it gets too late."

After I'd sneaked the dinosaurs back into the house we ran off toward Banky and Larry Dunn's secret fort.

It wasn't until nine o'clock at night when I was in bed that a bell went off in my head. I'd forgotten all about the radioactive dinosaurs!

I put on my tennis shoes, got my night-reading flashlight, climbed out the back window and went down the tree into the backyard. I got to the battleground and saw the three radioactive graves, but when I moved the rock on the first one and dug a little bit down I didn't hit one dinosaur, not one! The second grave was empty too. I didn't even move the rock from the third one, I just sat there and felt real stupid.

I couldn't help thinking about Sunday school again. I remembered the story about how a bunch of angels came down and rolled away the rock that was in front of Jesus's grave to let him go to heaven. I think it took them three days to push the rock far enough so he could squeeze out. My dinosaurs weren't even in their graves for three hours before someone rolled their rocks away. Maybe it was a lot easier for a bunch of angels to get a million dinosaurs to heaven than it was to get the saver of the whole world there, but I wished they'd given me a couple more hours.

But I was just making excuses to myself for being so stupid. I know if a detective had looked at these rocks

41

he wouldn't have found a clue of a single angel being there, but I'd bet a million bucks that he'd have seen that those rocks were covered with a ton of LJ Jones fingerprints.

I never played with LJ again after that. So playing with Rufus got to be O.K. It was a lot better not to have to worry about getting stuff stolen when you were with your friends, and it was a lot better not spending half the time arguing about who's going to be the Nazi dinosaurs.

I was wrong when I said that me and Rufus being near each other all the time would make people tease both of us twice as much. People started leaving me alone and going right after Rufus. It was easy for them to do 'cause he was kind of like me, he had two things wrong with him too.

The first thing wrong with Rufus was the way he talked. After he said that "Hiya, y'all" stuff on the bus he got to be famous for it and no matter how much he tried to talk in a different way people wouldn't let him forget what he'd said.

The other thing wrong with him was his clothes. It didn't take people too long before they counted how many pairs of pants and shirts Rufus and Cody had. That was easy to do because Rufus only had two shirts and two pairs of pants and Cody only had three shirts and two pairs of pants. They also had one pair of blue jeans that they switched off on; some days Rufus wore them and some days Cody rolled the legs up and put them on. It's really funny how something as stupid as a pair of blue jeans can make you feel real, real bad but that's what happened to me.

We had been sort of secret friends for a couple of weeks before people really started getting on them about not having a bunch of clothes. Me and Rufus and Cody were on the bus right behind the driver one day when Larry Dunn walked up to our seat and said, "Country Corn Flake, I noticed how you and the Little Flake switch off on them pants, and I know Fridays is your day to wear 'em, but I was wonderin' if the same person who gets to wear the pants gets to wear the drawers that day too?"

Of course the whole bus started laughing and hollering. Larry Dunn went back to his seat real quick before the driver had a chance to tell anybody the secret he knew about Larry's momma. I looked over at Cody. He had the blue jeans on today and was pulling the waist out to check out his underpants.

Maybe it was because everybody else was laughing, maybe it was because Cody had such a strange look on his face while he peeked at his underpants, maybe it was because I was glad that Larry hadn't jumped on me, but whatever the reason was I cracked up too.

Rufus shot a look at me. His face never changed but I knew right away I'd done something wrong. I tried to squeeze the rest of my laugh down.

Things got real strange. Instead of Rufus jabbering away at me a mile a minute in school he scooted around in his seat so all I could see was his back. He didn't follow me out on the playground either, and he acted like he didn't want my sandwiches anymore. Ever since Momma had met Rufus and I told her about sharing my sandwiches with him she had been giving me four sandwiches and three apples for lunch. When I saw him and Cody weren't going to come under the swing at lunchtime I set the bag with their sandwiches and apples in it on the swing set. The bag was still there when the bell rang.

They quit sitting next to me on the bus too, and Rufus didn't show up that night to play. After this junk went on for three or four days I sneaked the pillowcase full of dinosaurs out and headed over to where Rufus lived. I knocked on the door and Cody answered. I thought things might be back to being O.K. because Cody gave me a great big smile and said, "Hiya, Kenny, you wanna talk to Rufus?"

"Hi, Cody."

"Just a minute."

Cody closed the door and ran back inside. A minute later Rufus came to the door.

"Hey, Rufus, I thought you might want to play dinosaurs. It's your turn to be the Americans."

Rufus looked at the pillowcase, then back at me. "I ain't playin' with you no more, Kenny."

"How come?" I knew, though.

"I thought you was my friend. I didn't think you was like all them other people," he said. "I thought you was different." He didn't say this stuff like he was mad, he just sounded real, real sad. He pulled Cody out of the doorway and shut it.

Rufus might as well have tied me to a tree and said, "Ready, aim, fire!" I felt like someone had pulled all my teeth out with a pair of rusty pliers. I wanted to knock on his door and tell him, "I *am* different," but I was too embarrassed so I walked the dinosaurs back home.

I couldn't believe how sad I got. It's funny how things could change so much and you wouldn't notice. All of a sudden I started remembering how much I hated riding the bus, all of a sudden I started remembering how lunchtime under the swing set alone wasn't very much fun, all of a sudden I started remembering that before Rufus came to Flint my only friend was the world's biggest dinosaur thief, LJ Jones, all of a sudden I remembered that Rufus and Cody were the only two kids in the whole school (other than Byron and Joey) that I didn't automatically look at sideways.

A couple of days later Momma asked me to sit in the kitchen with her for a while.

"How's school?"

"O.K." I knew she was fishing to find what was wrong and hoped it wouldn't take her too long. I wanted to tell her what I'd done.

"Where's Rufus been? I haven't seen him lately."

It was real embarrassing but tears just exploded out of my face and even though I knew she was going to be disappointed in me I told Momma how I'd hurt Rufus's feelings.

"Did you apologize?"

"Sort of, but he wouldn't let me talk to him."

"Well, give him some time, then try again."

"Yes, Momma."

The next day after school when the bus pulled up at Rufus's stop Momma was standing there. When Rufus and Cody got off they said, "Hi, Mrs. Watson," and gave her their big smiles. The three of them walked toward Rufus's house. Momma put her hand on Rufus's head while they walked.

Momma didn't say anything when she got home and I didn't ask her but I kept my eye on the clock. At exactly five-thirty there was a knock and I knew who it was and I knew what I had to do.

Momma and Joey were in the living room and when they heard the knock everything there got real quiet. Rufus and Cody were standing on the porch smiling a mile a minute. I said, "Rufus, I'm sorry."

He said, "That's O.K."

I wasn't through, though. I really wanted him to know. "I *am* different."

He said, "Shoot, Kenny, you think I don't know? Why you think I came back? But remember, you said it's my turn to be the Americans."

People started moving around in the living room again. I guess I should have told Momma that I really appreciated her helping me get my friend back but I didn't have to. I was pretty sure she already knew.

4. Froze—Up Southern Folks

Because she'd been born in Alabama, Momma didn't really know anything about the cold. Even though she'd lived in Flint for fifteen years she still thought cold weather could kill you in a flash. That's why me and Joey were the warmest kids at Clark Elementary School. Momma wouldn't let us go out on a cold winter day unless we were wearing a couple of T-shirts, a couple of sweaters, a couple of jackets and a couple of coats, plus gigantic snow pants that hung on your shoulders by suspenders, plus socks and big, black, shiny rubber boots that closed with five metal buckles.

We wore so many clothes that when we pulled our final coat on we could barely bend our arms. We wore so many clothes that when Byron wasn't around, the other kids said stuff like "Here come some of them Weird Watsons doing their Mummy imitations." But the worst part of this was having to take all this stuff off once we got to school.

It was my job to make sure Joey got out of her coats

and things O.K., so after I took all of my junk off I went down to the kindergarten and started working on hers.

Joey usually looked like a little zombie while I peeled the coats and jackets off of her. She got so hot inside all this stuff that when I finally got down to the last layer she'd be soaking wet and kind of drowsy-looking.

I took her hood off and unwrapped the last scarf that was around her head. When that last scarf came off there was always a real nice smell, like Joey was a little oven and inside all these clothes she'd baked up her own special perfume, with the smell of shampoo and soap and the pomade Momma put in her hair. That was the only part I didn't mind. I loved sticking my nose right on top of Joey's head and smelling all those nice things baked together.

Momma always kept a little towel in Joey's last jacket's pocket so I could make sure her face and hair were dry.

"Kenny," she said one time while I wiped the sweat from her forehead and hair, "can't you do something to stop Mommy from making us get so hot?"

"I tried, Joey. Momma thinks she's protecting us from the cold." I started trying to get Joey's shoes out of her boots. Whoever invented these boots should be shot because once the boots got ahold of your shoes they wouldn't let them go for anything. I pulled everything off Joey's foot and gave her the boot while I reached my hand inside to tug on the shoe. We pulled and pulled but it seemed like the harder we pulled, the harder the boot sucked the shoe back in.

"Maybe Byron'll help make Mommy stop if we let him know how hot we get."

Joey was too young to understand that Byron didn't care about anything but himself He was kind of nice to her, though, and didn't treat her like he treated me and other kids.

We tugged and tugged and the shoe started coming out an inch at a time. Finally it made that funny sound like water going down the drain and slid out of the boot.

"Whew!" I tied Joey's shoes back on her feet and used her towel to wipe my own forehead. I couldn't wait until I was old enough to not listen to what Momma told me.

The next morning Momma was burying Joey in all her clothes again. Joey was doing the usual whining and complaining. "Mommy, can't I wear just one jacket, I get too hot! And besides, when I wear all this junk I'm the laughing sock of the morning kindergarten."

Momma's hand came up to cover her mouth but she got serious when she said, "Joey, I don't want you to be the laughing 'sock,' but I don't want you catching a cold. You've got to keep bundled up out there, it's colder than you think. This cold is very dangerous, people die in it all the time."

Joey pouted and said, "Well, if they die in it all the time how come we don't see any frozen people when we go to school?"

Momma gave Joey a funny look and pulled her hood

over her head. "Sweetheart, do what Mommy says, it's better to be too warm than too cold."

Joey whined a little more while Momma put her boots on her. Me and Byron went outside and waited on the porch. He was trying to look cool but I said to him anyway, "Man, I hate taking all that stuff off Joey when we get to school, she whines and cries the whole time." I stood next to him and looked at him sideways.

"Seems to me like you got a real bad memory. Who you think took all that stuff off your little behind all these years? What goes around goes around."

I was surprised he'd said anything, since Byron thought it was cool not to answer stuff when someone younger than you said it. But he wasn't being completely nice. While I was talking he kept moving around me so if I wanted to look at him sideways I'd have to move too. It must have looked like we were doing some kind of square dance with me moving around like one foot was nailed to the porch.

"Yeah, but I didn't cry and whine."

Byron kept circling me and put his hand behind his ear. "What? I know you didn't say what I think you said. You were the cryingest little clown there ever was."

With Byron walking around me like that we must have looked like we were in the Wild West and I was a wagon train and Byron was the Indians circling, waiting to attack.

Byron changed directions and started going around the other way, and I acted like my other foot was nailed to the porch and started following him sideways that way.

I knew there wasn't much point saying a whole bunch more to him, so I said mostly to myself, "Man, I hate listening to Joey whining when I take all that junk off her at school."

"Well, listen here," he said, "I'ma help you out."

I know it's kind of stupid to think that someone who's teasing you by going around in circles is going to help you out but I said anyway, "How?"

He kept going round and round me. I bet we looked like the solar system, with me being the sun and Byron being the orbiting Earth.

"I'll talk to Joey. You know, kinda put her mind at ease."

This didn't sound too good, and I got sick of By teasing me so I let the Earth orbit by itself.

Joey finally came out and the three of us walked toward the bus stop.

Byron started right in. "Baby Sis, I know you don't like wearing all them clothes, right?"

"Right, Byron, they get too hot!"

"Yeah, I'm hip, but you know there's a good reason why you gotta have all that stuff on."

"Why? Only me and Kenny wear this much junk."

"Yeah, but what you don't know is that Momma's only doing what's right, there's something she don't want you two to know yet, but I know you some real mature kids so I'ma tell you anyway."

"O.K., tell us."

I wanted to know too. Even though I was in fourth grade I fell for a lot of the stuff Byron came up with. He made everything seem real interesting and important.

"All right, but when Momma finally do tell you guys this stuff you gotta act like you surprised, deal?"

Both me and Joey said, "Deal!"

Byron looked around to make sure no one was listening, then said, "Have you ever noticed early in the morning some of the time you wake up and hear garbage trucks?"

"Yeah."

"And have you noticed how when you get up and go to school you almost never see them trucks?"

"Yeah."

"And have you ever noticed how when you do see one of them trucks it got a real big door in the back of it that opens and shuts so you can't see what's inside?"

"Yeah."

"And have you noticed how that door is too big for even the biggest garbage can in the world?"

"Yeah."

"And Joey, did you notice how Momma got kind of nervous and didn't answer your question about not seeing people being frozed up on the street?"

"Yeah."

Byron looked around and made us get real close to him.

"O.K., now this is the part you gonna have to look surprised at when Momma tells you about it, but before

I tell you you gonna have to practice acting surprised so I don't get in trouble for letting you know, O.K.?"

"Yeah!"

"Kenny, you first."

I made my eyes get real big and threw my mouth open.

"Not bad, but try it with some sound."

I made my eyes get real big, threw my mouth open and said, "What the . . . ?"

"Perfect. Baby Sis, your turn."

Joey did exactly what I did.

"That's good, but I think we need some action. Do all that stuff and throw your arms up like you just heard some real shocking stuff."

We did.

"Cool, now do it together, three times. Go."

Me and Joey did it three times, then Byron said, "Listen real careful." He looked around to make sure the coast was clear. "There's a good reason Momma makes you all wear all them clothes, and it's got to do with them big doors on the back of the garbage trucks, dig?"

Me and Joey nodded our heads the best we could with all of those clothes on.

"You see, some of them trucks ain't real garbage trucks at all. Joey, you was right, every cold morning like this the streets is full of dead, froze people. Some of the time they freeze so quick they don't even fall down, they just stand there froze solid!"

Joey was believing every word. I wasn't too sure.

"But you notice that not everybody gets froze like that, it's just them folks from down South who got that thin, down-home blood who freeze so quick. And you know Momma ain't from Flint, she grew up in Alabama and that means half of y'all's blood is real thin, so Momma's worried that one morning it's gonna be cold enough to freeze you all.

"That's where them fake garbage trucks come in. Every morning they go round picking the froze folks off the street, and they need them big doors because someone who got froze don't bend in the middle and they wouldn't fit in no regular ambulance."

Joey looked like she was hypnotized. Her mouth was open and her eyes were bugging.

"But both of you gotta swear never, ever to try and look in the back of one of them trucks. I did it once and I'ma tell you, there ain't nothin' more horrible than seein' hundreds of dead, froze-up Southern folks crammed up inside a garbage truck. It's a sight that I'ma carry to my grave with me. So Joey, don't be cryin' and whinin' when you put all them clothes on, it would break my heart to see my own family froze solid so's they got throwed in one them fake garbage trucks."

Joey started crying.

Byron told me, "Give my regards to Clark, Poindexter," and left me there to wipe Joetta's tears. I've got to admit, Joey didn't do any more whining when she had to get into her winter clothes.

———

The only good thing about Momma being afraid of the cold was that we were the only kids at Clark who got to wear real leather gloves.

Most of the other kids had to wear cheap plastic mittens that would start to crack up after two or three snowball fights or one real cold day. Some of them had to wear socks on their hands and some of them just had to scrunch their arms up in the sleeves of their jackets. But Momma made sure we got real leather gloves with real rabbit's fur on the inside of them, and I'm not bragging, but we got to go through two pairs a year each!

At the end of every winter Momma and Dad would go downtown to Montgomery Ward's when gloves were going on sale and buy six pairs for us kids. The only problem with having two pairs of gloves was that if you lost one pair you had to wear the next pair kindergarten-style. That meant Momma would run a string through the sleeves of your coat and tie two safety pins on the ends of the string, then she'd pin your gloves to the string and it was impossible to lose the gloves because every time you took them off they'd just hang from your coat.

I pulled a trick on Momma to help Rufus. For a while I shared my first pair of gloves with him. I'd keep the right hand glove and he'd keep the left hand one, that way we both could get in snowball fights and, instead of Rufus scrunching both of his hands up in his sleeves, I'd scrunch one of mine and he'd scrunch one of his. This was O.K. for a while but then I figured that if I told Momma I'd lost my first pair she'd give me the second one and me and Rufus each would have a full pair of gloves.

It worked! Momma put the second pair on my coat kindergarten-style and warned me, "This is the last one, Kenny, after this you won't have anything for the rest of the year so be very careful." I just about broke out laughing when she held me by the arms and looked right in my eyes and said, "Do you know what frostbite will do to you?"

"Yes, Momma." I looked sad on the outside but on the inside I was feeling great. I gave Rufus the right hand glove and everything was fine, for about a week.

That's when my second pair of gloves, kindergarten string, safety pins and all, disappeared out of the closet at school.

Rufus had to let me borrow one of my old gloves back and we were back to scrunching one hand each up in our coat sleeves, but since Rufus was now the official owner of the gloves he got to keep the right hand one and I had to wear the left hand one.

Two days later Larry Dunn stopped wearing socks on his hands and started wearing a pair of real leather gloves with real rabbit fur on the inside of them. The only difference between my old gloves and Larry's new ones was that mine had been brown and Larry's were black.

Me and Rufus found this out when Larry ran up behind us and said, "This is Friday, y'all, time to do the laundry. Who's gonna be first? Country Corn Flake? Cockeye Kenny?"

He didn't wait for us to make up our minds and grabbed me first. He said to Rufus, "If you run away during Cockeye's wash I'ma hunt you down and hurt you bad, boy. This ain't gonna take but a minute so just stick around." Rufus stood there looking worried.

Larry wasn't like other bullies; he wasn't happy taking a handful of snow and smashing it in your face and running off. Larry gave what he called Maytag Washes.

With a Maytag Wash you had to go through all of the different cycles that a washing machine did, and even though when Larry gave you a Maytag all of the cycles were exactly the same, each part had a different name and the wash wasn't done until you went through the final spin and had snow in every part of your face.

Ever since Larry got these new leather gloves he was giving *Super* Maytag Washes because he could grind a whole lot more snow in your face for a whole lot longer since his hands weren't getting as cold.

Larry was tearing me up, I was crying even before the first rinse cycle was done and he finally let me go. After he washed Rufus up we started walking home and Rufus said, "Man, he stole your gloves."

Who didn't know this? But you couldn't prove it, and besides, my old gloves were brown and Larry's new ones were black. "Uh-uh, mine were brown," I said.

Rufus dug a chunk of snow out of his jacket and said, "Look!"

The snow was covered with black, so was all of the snow I pulled out of my outer coat. Larry Dunn had stolen my gloves, then painted them black with shoe polish!

I didn't know what to do. Sooner or later Momma was going to notice I only had one glove, and ever since I'd found out that half of my blood was that thin Southern kind I'd started wondering if frostbite really could do some damage to my hands. I couldn't help myself, I sat on the curb and sniffled a couple of times, and finally cried. Rufus knew this was some real embarrassing stuff so he sat down beside me, looked the other way and acted like he didn't see me crying.

That's how come we didn't see By and Buphead walk up on us, I was too busy looking down trying not to be too obvious about crying and Rufus was too busy pretending he didn't notice that I was.

"What you cryin' about, punk?"

I made the mistake of telling Byron about my gloves and Larry Dunn.

"Where's he at?"

"Washing kids' faces over by the school."

"Come on."

Me and Rufus followed By and Buphead over to Clark. Larry Dunn was giving a Super Maytag to a fifth-grader. Byron interrupted the final rinse cycle and said, "Lemme see them gloves."

Larry Dunn said, "I ain't."

By snatched Larry Dunn's windbreaker with one hand, then touched his own mouth with his other hand.

"Buphead, I thought for sure when I got up this morning that my lips was working fine, and now when I feel 'em like this they still seem like they movin' just right. But if they working fine, how come this little fool ain't doing what I told him to do?"

Buphead shrugged and said, "Maybe the boy's ears is bad."

"Maybe. Maybe I'ma have to use deaf-people language to talk to him. Maybe I'ma have to talk to him like that woman in *The Miracle Worker*."

All the Weird Watsons had seen that show together and the way they talked to deaf people in that movie wasn't anything like the way Byron was talking to Larry Dunn. Byron's style of deaf-language was just to yell real loud and slap the side of Larry's head after each word.

"Lemme!" *Whack!* "See!" *Whack!* "Them!" *Whack!* "Gloves!" *Whack!* "Young!" *Whack!* "Fool!" *Whack-whackwhack!*

This had to be killing Larry Dunn.

Larry didn't cry or anything, he just stared at By and said, "I ain't."

He talked real tough but he didn't do a thing when Byron snatched the gloves off of his hands.

The palms of the gloves were brown and the backs were black. Byron threw me the gloves. "Here, Kenny."

"Thanks, By." That would have been fine with me but Byron wasn't through.

"Come here, Kenny."

I went and stood where Byron still had the neck of

Larry Dunn's skinny little windbreaker wadded up in his fist.

"Pop him," Byron said.

I gave Larry Dunn a slap on the arm.

"I'ma only tell you one more time. Pop him."

I hit Larry a little harder. I hoped he'd bend over and act like I'd killed him but he stood there trying to look cool.

Byron kept his word and only told me that one time, then when I didn't hit Larry hard enough, By punched me in the stomach. Hard! I didn't even feel it because I had all those sweaters and jackets and coats on, but I had more sense than Larry, I acted like I'd been popped by Sugar Ray Robinson and staggered around, then fell on my knees holding my stomach. I said, "*Uggggh . . .*"

A little crowd of kids started bunching up around us and Byron decided it was time to put on a show.

I don't know why bullies always have such a good sense of humor, but they do. Unless you were the one who was in the machine, you'd probably think that Larry Dunn's Maytag Washes were pretty funny. And unless it was your jacket that was balled up in Byron's fist with a crowd of kids bunching up, you'd have to say he was pretty funny too.

I knew Byron wasn't trying to help me anymore. He was just being mean.

"Well, well, well, Mr. Dunn," By said. "Today's your lucky day!"

By dragged Larry over to the chain-link fence that went all the way around Clark.

"You wanna know why you so lucky today?"

Larry Dunn didn't say anything so Byron grabbed his hair and jerked his head up and down a couple of times. "I guess that means yes."

The crowd of kids was getting bigger and bigger and was loving this. Not because they wanted to see Larry Dunn get jacked up, but because they wanted to see anybody get it, they'd have been just as happy if it was me or Rufus or someone else.

"Well, today's your lucky day 'cause I'm about to make a new movie and guess what, you gonna be the star!"

Byron jerked Larry's arms over his head three times. Larry Dunn was really tough! Not only because he wasn't crying when By was going to mess him up, but also because when Byron jerked his arms over his head like that we all could see that Larry's skinny little windbreaker was ripped under both arms and Larry just had on a T-shirt underneath it. You'd have to be pretty tough to stand around giving people Maytags on a day as cold as this with those skimpy clothes on!

"Hmmm, I guess that means you real excited about bein' in my flick. Yeah," By said, "but I got some even better news for you."

By lifted Larry up in the air and threw him. Larry landed on his butt.

Someone shouted, "Look at them shoes!" The crowd cracked up.

Larry Dunn's tennis shoes had holes in the bottoms

and he'd put pieces of a cardboard box in them to cover the holes.

Byron snatched him back to his feet.

"Look at that, you so excited 'bout being in my movie that you jumping for joy! Don't you even want to know what the flick's about?"

Larry's head got jerked up and down again.

"O.K., it's called *The Great Carp Escape*."

I hated watching this. Byron was the only person in the world who could make you feel sorry for someone as mean as Larry Dunn.

The Great Carp Escape was about a carp that was trying to get out of a net in the Flint River. The stupid fish would run into the net, get knocked down, then get back up and run into the net all over again.

Since he was the star, Larry Dunn had to play the carp and the fence around Clark was the net. The director of the movie, Byron, didn't like the way the scene was going and made the carp redo it over and over again.

"Let's see a little more fins this time, carp," Byron would say, then throw Larry into the fence. Since tennis shoes don't have a lot of grip on the ice, Larry would go into the fence hard and couldn't control what part of him hit first. I knew it really had to hurt to catch yourself on that cold fence with nothing on your hands, not even socks, but Larry Dunn was real, real tough, he had a bloody nose and still didn't cry.

I wished I hadn't told Byron about what happened, I wished I just could have gone the rest of the year with one glove. I couldn't stand to see how the movie was going to end, so me and Rufus left.

I could hear the *jink-jink* sound of that carp hitting the net and the screams and laughs of the audience from half a block away.

5. Nazi Parachutes Attack America and Get Shot Down over the Flint River by Captain Byron Watson and His Flamethrower of Death

Byron got caught lighting matches again and it looked like this time Momma was going to do what she always said she would. That's when Joetta turned on the tears and cried and begged so much that Momma let him off. She swore to him, though, that the next time he got caught starting fires she was going to burn him.

She told us that same sad old story about how when she was a little girl her house caught on fire and for two years after that she and her brothers had to wear clothes that smelled like smoke. Even though the story made Momma and Joey get all sad and sobby it was kind of funny to me and By. We'd heard it so many times that Byron even gave it a name. He called it Momma's Smokey the Bear story.

"I won't have you putting this family in danger. Just once more, Byron Watson, one more time and you're burned." Then, to show Byron how serious she was,

Momma raised her right hand and said, "I swear that with God as my witness!"

By got put on punishment for a month, but even before a week was gone he started up again.

I was up in the bedroom looking at comic books when I heard Byron go into the bathroom and lock the door. I knew something was up, since he only locked the door when he had something to hide.

I sneaked to the bathroom door and peeked through the keyhole. By was pretending he was making a movie called *Nazi Parachutes Attack America and Get Shot Down over the Flint River by Captain Byron Watson and His Flamethrower of Death*.

I could see that he'd made a bunch of little toilet paper parachutes and when he yelled, "Action!" he set one of them on fire and dropped it over the toilet. The guy in the Nazi parachute screamed as he floated down in flames and landed in the water with a loud hiss. Before the parachutist was dead By would flush the toilet and the Nazi would go down the drain going, "*Glub, glub, glub!*"

When the water was swirling him away Byron said the only Nazi talk that he knew, "Ya hold mine fewer, off we der same!"

Peeking through the keyhole, I could see Byron salute to the parachute when he flushed the toilet. "Such a brave soldier deserves our respect," he said, "so we give him a burial at sea."

The toilet stopped glugging and Byron said, "Not

bad, but let's have a little more screaming on the way down and how about having the Flamethrower of Death turned up a little bit?"

He picked up another toilet paper parachute, lit two matches at the same time, set the parachute on fire, yelled, "Take two!" and sent the next Nazi screaming into the toilet. Byron was on take seven when Momma finally wondered why the toilet was being flushed so much and came upstairs to see what was going on. The whole upstairs smelled like a giant match and she knew something was fishy even before she got to the top step.

She moved so quick and quiet that I still had my eyeball in the keyhole when she stepped into the hallway. I looked up and there she was.

"Momma, I . . ."

I knew I was going to get it for not turning Byron in but before I could say anything else Momma pushed me out of the way and hit the bathroom door with her shoulder like Eliot Ness, the cop on that *Untouchables* TV show!

The door jumped out of her way and banged into the bathtub, Byron turned around and screamed, Nazi number seven hit the water with a hiss, Byron threw his hands up in the air and said, "Momma, I—," Momma snatched Byron's neck and, stopping just to pick up the matches that Byron had dropped, she dragged him all the way down the stairs!

I could see that Momma had forgotten all about me

so I followed right behind. As they went down, By's feet touched the steps only one or two times. He looked like one of those ballerinas that dance just on the tips of their toes. Momma had her hand around his throat like it was a baseball bat and was holding him up in the air. I never knew Momma was so strong!

They danced into the living room and Joey started looking nervous. She ran over and huddled up next to me.

Momma's eyes got slitty with the eyeballs shooting around from side to side. It was almost too scary to watch but I kept looking since I knew there was going to be some real big action this time! Joey grabbed ahold of my arm and said, "What's going on, what'd he do?" She was starting to get jumpy because she'd never seen Momma so mad either.

I felt kind of sorry for Byron because Momma hadn't let go of his neck and, even though he was a lot older, we could tell he was just as scared as me and Joetta. He kept pretending he was Daddy Cool, though, and the only way you could tell he was scared to death was by looking at his eyes.

Momma kept her hand on Byron's neck and pushed him down on the couch and stood right in front of him. She opened the hand that hadn't been choking him and looked at the matches she'd picked up off the bathroom floor.

While one hand had been strangling Byron the other hand had been strangling the matches! The matches were soaking wet because whenever Momma got scared or nervous or mad her hands got real sweaty and disgusting.

Momma's voice got strange, hissing like a snake.

"Joetta, go out to the kitchen and bring me a book of matches."

"But Mommy . . . ," Joey said, starting to get all sobby.

"Joetta, do what I told you."

"Mommy, I can't . . ." The tears really started coming and Joey was squeezing my arm.

"Joetta, go get those matches!"

"Please, Mommy, he won't do it again, will you, Byron? Promise her, promise Mommy you won't do it again!"

"Kenneth." She turned to me then. "Go get some matches."

This is what I was afraid of. If I didn't go get the matches I was going to be in worse trouble then I already was with Momma, and if I did go get the matches I knew Byron would kill me as soon as he got back from the hospital.

"Momma, I—"

"Move, young man!"

"Momma, wait a minute, I can't move, Joey's got me by the arm and if I move—"

Momma pointed her finger at Byron and said, "Don't you move a muscle." We all could tell Momma was super-mad 'cause she started talking in that real Southern-style accent.

Byron nodded his head and Momma let go of his throat and stormed into the kitchen.

Old Mr. Cool still had great big bug eyes and as soon as Momma's hand left his neck his own hands came up and started choking him themselves.

"Ooh, Byron, you better get out of here, go down to Buphead's until Dad gets home, he's probably gonna whip you, but Momma's really gonna burn you!" I told him.

"Please, Byron, run! Get out of here." Joey let go of my arm and ran over to Byron and tried to pull his fingers from around his throat. "Can't you tell, she's not playing!"

Joey kept pulling at his hand but it looked like Byron was hypnotized and he wouldn't move.

We all nearly jumped through the roof when the snake-woman voice came back into the room and said, "Joetta, move away from him."

Momma was carrying a piece of paper towel, a jar of Vaseline and a Band-Aid in one hand and a fresh, dry book of matches in the other.

She wasn't even going to take him to the hospital! She was going to set him on fire, then patch him up right at home!

Joetta saw the Vaseline and went crazy.

"Oh no, Mommy, let Daddy whip him, please, please!" Joey began pulling her braids and stamping her feet up and down. "Please don't set him on fire. . . ."

Her face was all wet and twisted up and she looked like a real nut.

It was hard to do, but I kind of felt sorry for Byron, though not too sorry because I knew he deserved whatever happened, first because he had a chance to escape and didn't take it and second because he was being a bad influence on me. *Nazi Parachutes Attack America and Get Shot Down over the Flint River by Captain Byron Watson and His Flamethrower of Death* looked like a real cool movie for me to make too. If Momma just gave Byron some stupid punishment, then maybe it would be worth it for me to flush some Nazis down the drain myself. But if you got set on fire for doing it the movie wasn't worth making.

So while I felt sorry for Byron because of what was going to happen to him I did want to see if Momma would keep her word and I always wondered what part of him she'd burn. His face? His hair? Maybe she'd just scare him by setting his clothes on fire while he was in them. But if she was just going to set his clothes on fire why did she need Vaseline? I knew Momma was going for skin!

"Joetta, move away." Momma's voice still sounded strange.

Joey spread her arms out to the side like a traffic cop and stood between Momma and Byron. "No, Mommy, wait . . ."

Momma gently set Joey to the side but Joetta kept hopping back with her arms spread to protect Daddy Cool.

They wrestled like this a couple of times before

Momma finally set all the burning equipment down and sat on the coffee table and pulled Joey into her lap.

She wiped Joey's stupid tears away with the paper towel and rocked her back and forth a couple of times going, "Shhh, honey, shhh."

When Joey finally stopped crying and blew her nose Momma said, "Sweetheart, I'm so proud of you, I know you're trying to protect your brother and that's a good thing, I know you don't want to see him get hurt, right?"

Joey sniffed and said, "No, Mommy."

"But honey, some of the time Momma has to do things she doesn't want to do. Now you really don't think I want to hurt Byron, do you?"

Joey had to think about this, the matches and the first aid stuff and the crazy look Momma had in her eyes made it seem like hurting Byron was exactly what Momma wanted to do.

After Joey didn't say anything Momma had to answer the question herself. "No, dear, Momma doesn't want to hurt Byron, but I don't want you going to school smelling like smoke either, and I don't want to see you or Kenneth or Daddy or Blackie or Tiger or Flipper or Flapper get burned up either. And if that boy"— Momma's voice got strange again and we all looked over at Byron, who was still being held on the couch by his own hands—"if that boy sets this house on fire with his nonsense I don't know what I'm gonna do." Momma's real voice was coming back. "So, Joetta, don't you see how Momma has to help Byron understand how dangerous and painful fire can be? Don't you see we've tried everything and nothing seems to get through that rock head of his?"

Joetta thought about her stupid cat and goldfish getting burned up and looked kind of hard over at Byron.

"But look at him, Mommy, he's really, really scared this time, maybe he won't—"

"Joetta, he's not that scared. Yet." Then Momma dropped the bomb on Joey. "Besides, don't you remember, sweetheart? Don't you remember when this happened last week I swore to God that if Byron did it again I would burn him? What do you think, do you think I should break my word to God?"

Joey was at the age when you're real religious. She went to Sunday school three days a week.

"Huh, honey, should I break my word to God?"

"No, Mommy," Joey said. Then she scrunched her face up like she was eating something sour and cried out, "Since you promised I guess you gotta do it." She took a giant breath, then sobbed, "Go ahead, burn him up!"

Joey climbed off Momma's lap and Byron's eyes got bigger and bigger but his traitor hands kept him pinned to the couch.

"But please, Mommy, don't burn him too bad, O.K., please, please?" Joey was starting up again.

"Don't worry, sweetheart, I won't. I'm just going to burn his fingers enough so he won't be tempted by fire ever again."

Those were like magic words; they snapped Byron right out of the spell Momma put on him. It was like his hands said, "Fingers? Did she say she was gonna burn someone's fingers?" Because when they found out it was them that were going to get burned they let go of Byron's throat and joined the rest of his body in deciding to wait at Buphead's until Dad got home.

Byron was fast.

Momma was faster.

He didn't even make it out of the living room before Momma tackled him. Momma sure is a good athlete!

She sat on his chest and said, "Not this time, buster, this time you pay." She said "bus-tuh."

Byron squirmed around for a second and then did something I'd only see him do a couple of times before. He started crying.

Momma lit a match and grabbed Byron by the wrist and said, "Put your finger out."

I couldn't believe it! By's finger popped right out! He was hypnotized all over again!

Momma's horrible snake-woman voice came out again and said, "If you ever, ever . . ." The match got closer and closer to Byron's skinny brown finger. ". . . play with—no, if you ever even look at . . ." Byron's hand was shaking and he was crying like a big baby but his finger still stayed out. ". . . another match in this house . . ." The match was getting closer and closer, and I knew Byron could feel the heat. ". . . I will personally, by myself . . ." It was so close now that I thought I could hear the sweat on

73

Byron's finger getting turned into steam and going *Pssss*!

". . . I will burn not just one finger, I will burn your entire hand, then send you to juvenile home!"

Byron closed his eyes and screamed. Right when the fire was going to give him a good roasting Joetta ran across the room and, sounding like that Little Engine That Thought It Could, she blew the match out before it got him! She thought she missed, though, 'cause she stood there huffing and puffing and patoohing at the match even after it went out. Momma's hand, Byron's finger and the match were soaked with Joey's slob.

"Honey, we agreed, didn't we?"

"Yes, Mommy," Joey looked down and said, "but I thought you got him."

"Not yet, sweetheart, but I'm going to."

Four more times Momma lit a match and four more times Joey patoohed them out. Finally Momma got sick of having slob all over her hand and gave up. That night Byron had to deal with Dad. No picnic, but a lot better ending to his Nazi parachutes movie than *Captain Byron Watson Gets Captured and Burned Alive by the Evil Snake Woman with His Own Flamethrower of Death*.

6. Swedish Cremes and Welfare Cheese

Momma stuck her head into the living room and said, "Byron, I want you and Kenny to go up to Mitchell's and get some milk, a loaf of bread and a can of tomato paste for dinner." She waved a little piece of paper at us that had the grocery list written on it.

"How come Kenny can't go by hisself?"

"Byron, I want a half gallon of milk, a loaf of bread and a small can of tomato paste."

If you asked Momma why you had to do something and she didn't feel like explaining she just repeated herself. She was chopping up onions for spaghetti sauce and I guess the tears made it so she didn't feel like talking. If you were stupid enough to ask your question again there would be the loudest quiet in the world coming from Momma. If you went totally crazy and asked the question a third time you might as well tie yourself to a tree and say, "Ready, aim, fire!"

Byron got the message and jerked up off the couch

and walked over to the TV and punched the "Off" knob. I knew this wasn't going to be a fun walk up to Mitchell's. We went into the kitchen.

"Gimme the money."

"Just sign for it."

"Just what?"

"Just tell Mr. Mitchell you want to sign for it." Momma kept whacking the onions.

"What, just go in there and tell Mr. Mitchell I wanna sign for some food?"

"Your daddy and me made all the arrangements last weekend, Byron. Mr. Mitchell will let us sign for groceries until payday. Lots of people do it. A half gallon of milk, a loaf of bread and a small can of tomato paste." Momma started chopping the onions a little harder.

"So I ain't gotta give him no cash?"

Whack, whack, whack.

All of a sudden Byron's face jumped like a bell went off in his head. "Wait a minute! I know what this mean—we on welfare, ain't we?"

I held my breath. If I found out we were on welfare I was going to really have to get ready to be teased.

"No. We're not on welfare."

"I can't believe it. You really gonna start serving welfare food in this house? You really gonna make me go embarrass myself by signing a welfare list for some groceries like a blanged peon?"

I guess By hadn't been counting how many times Momma had repeated herself. She smacked the knife on the kitchen counter and jumped right up in By's face.

"Listen here, Mr. High and Mighty, since you just got to know, food is food. You've eaten welfare food in this house before and if need be you'll eat it again. Don't come playin' that nonsense with me. I already told you, this is not welfare food. You've got about five seconds to have that door hit you in the back. Kenny, move."

By pouted and walked real fast up to Mitchell's so I had to kind of run along to keep up with him.

He didn't say anything while we got the stuff Momma wanted, he just snatched the things off the shelves. Then he dropped the bomb on me. "You go get in line and hold our spot, I'ma look at some comics for a minute. When you get up to the register I'll come and tell 'em how we gonna pay."

Aww, man! I knew what that meant, By'd figured out a way not to get embarrassed. He was going to hide until after I'd signed for the groceries, I was going to be the one who got embarrassed. I couldn't argue or anything so now it was me who was pouting.

Byron disappeared around the comic-book rack.

"Hi, Kenny."

"Hi, Mr. Mitchell."

"This all you want?"

"Uh-huh." He took the groceries and rang them up on the cash register.

"That's a dollar and twenty-three cents." I saw By's head come peeking around the comics.

"Uh, this has gotta go on the welfare list," I said kind of quiet.

Mr. Mitchell twisted his face up. "On the what?"

I said real low so only Mr. Mitchell could hear, "We just found out we got put on welfare and we've gotta sign this food up on the welfare list." Byron's head disappeared again.

Mr. Mitchell laughed. "Kenny, this isn't a welfare list, it just means your daddy's gonna pay all at once instead of a few times every week."

"Really?"

Mr. Mitchell reached under the counter and opened up a little brown box. He pulled out a bunch of yellow cards and I could see "Watson" was written on the top of one of them. He wrote "$1.23" on the first line and said, "Sign here," then pointed to a spot next to the "$1.23." I wrote "Kenneth Watson" and gave him back the pen.

"That's it?"

"That's it." He put the groceries in a brown paper bag and handed them to me.

"See you, Mr. Mitchell."

The second I walked out of the store Byron was next to me and he was in a lot better mood.

"Man, I can't believe it! We just had a chance to get a bagful of free food and all we took was some stupid milk, a loaf of bread and a can of tomato sauce!"

Byron's good mood started getting to me too. He was smiling and even put his arm around my shoulder as we walked. I couldn't help myself, it felt so grown-up to have By walking with me like that, I started laughing right along with him.

His mood was so much better that he even took the bag of groceries from me. Most of the time when Momma made us go to Mitchell's, Byron would make me carry the bags from the store right up to the front porch. Then he'd take them from me so Momma would think he'd carried them the whole way. But now he started carrying them four blocks away from home!

"This is just too much, all you gotta do is sign that stupid card and that old fool Mitchell'll give you what you want! Too, too much!"

Now that By was happy, I had two questions I wanted to ask him. First, he'd said a word that I'd never heard before and since he said it in front of Momma I knew it wasn't cussing. As we walked home with his arm around my shoulder I thought I might get a real answer from him.

"Byron, what's a peon?"

"A peon? Didn't you see *The Magnificent Seven*? Peons was them folks what was so poor that the rich folks would just as soon pee on them as anything else."

I knew this had to be a lie. You could get yourself in a lot of trouble if you listened to half the stuff Byron said. But I asked my next question anyway. "What do you think the welfare food was that Momma said she gave us?" I wished I hadn't asked 'cause this brought back his bad mood.

He took his arm from around my shoulder and said, "I *know* what it was." He handed me back the groceries too.

"Don't you remember how some of the time Dad

sneaks up in the morning and goes in the kitchen and when he come out there's a big jug of milk? Ain't you ever wondered where that milk come from? You ever seen any udders on Dad? That milk come out of one of them big brown boxes they keep up on them high shelves, pure-D welfare food!

"And don't you remember that cheese? Who ever heard of cheese coming in a box as big as a loaf of bread? You ever try to pick one of them things up? Real cheese come in hunks or slices, not no blanged loaf that weigh forty pounds. I always thought there was something strange about that mess and now I know, she been sneaking us welfare food! Pure-D welfare food!"

The cheese tasted O.K. to me and, except for a big powdery lump every once in a while, Dad's milk was all right too. But to try to get Byron back into his good mood, I acted real disgusted and said, "Awww, man . . ."

A week later I was walking in the alley behind Mitchell's when a big cookie with pink frosting just about hit me in the head. It went by like a little flying saucer, then crashed in the dirt. I looked all around and didn't see anybody so I put my hands over my face and stood still because I knew if something weird like this happened once it usually happened again. Sure enough, another cookie hit me right in the back and a big laugh came out of the green-apple tree. Byron.

He dropped out of the tree like a superhero. He had a great big bag of cookies in one hand and a green apple with a giant bite out of it in the other.

"Want some?" By tipped the bag of Swedish Creme cookies at me. I knew this was a trick, the bag must have been empty, but I looked inside anyway. There was still a half a bag of cookies!

"Thanks!" I grabbed two of the cookies and looked at them real good in case By had put bugs or something on them. They were clean, but I still kept waiting for the trick. Why would Byron waste four good cookies on me?

Man! Swedish Cremes have got to be the best cookies in the world. I gulped them down and wiped my hands on my pants. I couldn't believe it, By tipped the bag at me again!

He jumped up and snatched a green apple off the tree, checked it for wormholes, then handed it to me. "You best eat some of this, them Swedish Cremes is good at first but they get kinda thick in your throat after while."

Byron was being too nice, so I knew something bad was about to happen. Then I noticed a crumpled-up Swedish Cremes bag on the ground next to the tree and I could figure out why he was being so generous. He'd already eaten a bag and a half.

A bell went off in my head. I knew now why he'd been so excited and happy when he found out about getting "free food" at Mitchell's. By was signing up for stuff that Momma and Dad didn't even know about!

It was like he read my mind, 'cause I was just about to say "Oooh, By . . ." when he stopped being friendly and crossed his eyes at me and said, "Don't even think about it, Poindexter, you ate two of 'em yourself so quit wastin' my cookies and just shut up and enjoy what's left." He tipped the bag at me again.

He had me. I couldn't tell on him, or else I'd be in just as much trouble as he would. I took another one.

By went over to the green-apple tree and slid his back against it until he was sitting down. I did the same thing right next to him and we sat together munching. I wasn't used to being this friendly with Byron so I guess I was kind of nervous and didn't really know what we should talk about. By just sat there chomping down apples, so I tried to think what him and Buphead would talk about when they sat around like this. Finally I said, "So By, how about you and me doing a little cussing?"

He twisted up his face and said, "I thought I told your narrow behind to shut your piehole and eat the stinkin' cookies. Now do it!"

I got a huge smile! Those aren't real cuss words but, man, they're close enough!

"Look!" By pointed up at a telephone wire where a big bird sat. The bird was about the size of a pigeon and was grayish brown with a long pointy tail hanging underneath it.

By jumped up and said, "That's a mourning dove, they're the coolest birds in the world, don't nothing shake them up!" By threw a Swedish Creme at it. The cookie zipped right by the bird's head and all the bird did was raise its wings once and look behind it.

He threw three more cookies at the bird and it still didn't move.

When Byron's fourth Swedish Creme left his hand I knew that if the bird didn't move he was going to get whacked. The cookie popped the bird smack-jab in the chest! The bird's wings both stuck out to the side and for a hot second with its tail hanging down and its wings sticking out like that it looked like a perfect small letter *t* stuck up on the telephone wire. Then, in slow motion, the bird leaned back and crashed to the dirt of the alley behind Mitchell's.

I'd been throwing rocks and things at birds since I was born and had never even come close to hitting one, I'd seen a million people throw a million things at birds and no one had ever really hit one, not even a pigeon! But now By had knocked a bird right out of the sky with a Swedish Creme cookie!

When I got to Byron he'd picked up the bird and was holding it in his hands. The bird's head drooped backward and was rolling from side to side. Dead as a donut.

"You got him! You got a bird!"

Byron held the bird in one hand and with his other one gently brushed pink frosting off of the dove's chest.

"You got him! I've never seen a bird get . . ."

I looked right at By and his face was all twisted up and his eyes were kind of shut. He dropped the bird, walked over to the green-apple tree and started throwing up.

I stood there with my mouth open, I couldn't believe Byron was starting to cry. And I couldn't believe how much vomit a bag and a half of Swedish Cremes and some green apples could make.

When it looked like he was done I walked over and put my hand on his back. As soon as I touched him, he popped me in the arm, hard!

"By, what—"

He picked up a rotten apple and threw it at me. "Get out of my face, clown. What you starin' at? Them apples got me sick, you little cross-eyed punk! Get out of here."

Rotten apples started coming at me real hard and fast so I left.

It was hard to understand what was going on with Byron. Some of the time if a genie came and gave you three wishes you wouldn't mind using all three of them to wish some real bad stuff on him. Not stupid things like that woman in the fairy tale when she wished her husband had a sausage on his nose either, I mean stuff that would make Byron hurt so much that he'd have to think every day about how mean he is.

If he just had a sausage growing off of his nose people might laugh at him behind his back but no one would have nerve enough to tease him to his face and call him Weenie-Nose or something. He wouldn't know how it feels to always have someone jumping on you, how sad that can make you get. Sometimes I hated him that much and thought he was the meanest person in the world.

After my arm quit hurting from his punch I went back to the alley behind Mitchell's to take another look at the dead bird but it was gone. Right in the spot where the bird had crashed By had dug a little grave, and on top of the grave there were two Popsicle sticks tied together in a cross.

Leave it to Daddy Cool to kill a bird, then give it a funeral. Leave it to Daddy Cool to torture human kids at school all day long and never have his conscience bother him but to feel sorry for a stupid little grayish brown bird.

I don't know, I really wished I was as smart as some people thought I was, 'cause some of the time it was real hard to understand what was going on with Byron.

7. Every Chihuahua in America Lines Up to Take a Bite out of Byron

I was sitting at the kitchen table doing homework and watching Momma make dinner when Byron came in through the back door. He was surprised we were there 'cause as soon as he saw us he turned around and tried to walk right back out.

Both me and Momma smelled a rat.

"Byron," Momma said, "what have I told you about wearing that hat in the house?"

"Oh yeah, I was just going right back . . ." He pushed the screen door open again.

"Wait a minute."

Byron was trapped in the doorway, with his right foot in and his left foot out.

"Come here."

Momma put down the knife she'd been peeling potatoes with and wiped her hands on a dish towel.

Byron's inside foot joined his outside one in trying to get away. "Uh, I'll be back in a minute, they're waiting for me down at—"

"Byron Watson, you take off that hat and get over here right this minute!" It was "he-uh" instead of "here." Uh-oh.

Byron started walking toward Momma in slow motion, sliding his feet on the linoleum. He pulled off his hat and stood there looking down, like his shoes were all of a sudden real interesting.

Byron's head was covered with a blue-and-white handkerchief.

Momma sucked in a ton of air. "What have you done?" We all knew, though. She took a step back and leaned against the counter like if it wasn't there she'd have fallen down. "Oh my God, your father will kill you!"

"He don't have no cause to."

"You've gone and done it, haven't you."

Byron kept his head down.

"Haven't you!" Momma yelled.

"Yes!" Byron yelled back.

Momma reached out and snatched the handkerchief off of By's head.

Me and Momma both went, "Huhhh!"

Byron had gotten a conk! A process! A do! A butter! A ton of trouble!

His hair was reddish brown, straight, stiff and slick-looking. Parts of it stuck straight up like porcupine stickers because Momma hadn't been too gentle when she snatched the handkerchief off.

He smoothed his hair back in place.

"Well," Momma said, "that's it, you are now at your

daddy's mercy. You've known all along how we feel about putting those chemicals in your hair to straighten it, but you decided you are a grown man and went and did it anyway." Momma was real hot, but she surprised me, she just shook her head and went back to peeling potatoes.

Byron stood there looking at his feet and I kept pretending I was doing homework.

Finally Momma slammed the knife down and turned around to look at By again. Byron stood perfectly still while Momma walked around him a couple of times taking a better look at his hair. This looked like the Indians circling the wagons again, but this time it was Byron who had to be the white people!

Finally Momma stopped and said, "But before your father gets to you, let me ask you something. What do you think? What do you think now that you've gone and done it? Does it make you look any better? Is this straight"—Momma flicked some more of Byron's hair back up porcupine-style—"is this straight mess more attractive than your own hair? Did those chemicals give you better-looking hair than me and your daddy and God gave you?"

It was strange, a little laugh was starting to get into Momma's voice. "Huh, what do you think?

"Well, Bozo," she said, flicking a piece of By's hair out over his left ear and then another piece out over his right one, "maybe you were planning on joining the circus, 'cause you sure do look like an honest-to-God clown now."

Momma was right. With big clumps of his hair sticking out to the side over his ears like that he really did look like Bozo. I broke out laughing, but Byron shot me a real dirty look and I stopped and looked back down at my math book. I hated it when things like that happened and my head automatically went down by itself!

"Why on earth would you do this, Byron?"

"I wanted Mexican-style hair. I don't see nothing wrong with it."

When he saw Momma just looking sad and me looking like I wanted to crack up again, Byron got kind of mad and said, "I think it's cool!"

"Well, Daddy Cool, you enjoy your Mexican-style hair while you can, 'cause I'm sure when your daddy gets through with you you won't be enjoying too much of anything, and cool is the one thing you won't be feeling.

"You just slide your cool self right on up those stairs to your bedroom and wait for him, Daddy-o."

Byron clomped up the stairs.

I told Joey about what happened as soon as our next-door neighbor, Mrs. Davidson, brought her home from Sunday school. Me and Joey went up to see Byron.

Byron was on the top bunk with his feet dangling over the side and his hands covering his face.

I loved times like this when Byron was about to really get it and couldn't pay me back for teasing him.

I started in on him as soon as me and Joey got into the room.

"Death row prisoner number five forty-one, you have a visitor.

"Please make this a short visit, ma'am, the priest will be here any minute to give the prisoner his last meal and his last cigarette. Oops! I forgot, no cigarettes for you, Five Forty-one, you've been banned from ever looking at matches, remember?"

Byron was feeling very sad. He didn't say anything to me, he didn't even give me a dirty look. That made me a lot braver.

When she saw his hair, Joetta's eyes got real big and her voice got all choky. "Byron Watson, what were you thinking about? Look at your head, Daddy's gonna kill you! Come down from there, let's go to the bathroom and wash that stuff out of your hair before Daddy gets here!"

Byron raised his slicked-down head from his hands. "Go away, Joey."

"Come on, Byron, we gotta wash your hair till that junk comes out, hurry!" Joetta pulled on Byron's dangling legs.

"Stop, Joey," he finally said. "This don't *wash* out, it's gotta *grow* out."

"You mean you have to keep it like that until it comes back normal?"

"Yeah," Byron said, kind of smiling. "They can't do nothin' to it till it grows back."

"Oh no! Daddy's gonna tear you up!"

I said, "That's right, ma'am, Five Forty-one is just

waiting for the executioner to get home. Would you like to stick around and write down his last words?"

Joey turned and snapped, "Why is this so funny to you, Kenny?" Her eyes looked real mean. "Who knows what Daddy is gonna do to him?"

Byron's hands came back up to cover his face.

I said to Joey, "Why are you yelling at me, it wasn't me who went and got a butter, and no one forced him to do it either." It makes me sick the way she's always protecting Byron.

She turned back to him. "Who did this to you, By?"

She didn't have to ask. There was only one other fourteen-year-old in the neighborhood who had a conk.

I answered for him. "It was Buphead."

"Why'd you let him, By?"

"I told you to go away, Joey."

"No, Byron, why'd you let him do this?"

"'Cause I wanted to, that's why."

"But didn't you know Mommy and Daddy would find out?"

"Shoot, you think I care what them squares say?"

I said, "And there you have it, ma'am, the reason Five Forty-one must die. He won't confess his guilt."

Byron looked at me for the first time and I started easing toward the door. He said, "You think I don't know what you're doing, punk? You think I don't know you're loving all this mess?

"But I been expecting this. This is just like that show

91

I seen about wolves. They said that the top-dog wolf is always getting challenged by jive little wolves. They said the top-dog wolf can't show no weakness at all, that if he do, if he gets hurt or something, if he steps on a broke bottle and starts limping or something, all the little jive wolves in the pack start trying to overthrow him. That's what's happening right now, you think I'm hurt and you and every other punk Chihuahua in America is climbing out of the woodwork to try and get a bite out of me.

"Lemme tell you something, when—"

We all heard the squeal of a car's brakes outside.

Joey and I ran over to the bedroom window that looked out to the street.

The Brown Bomber had just parked in front of the house.

Joey started blubbering.

Byron's legs dangled faster and faster.

Dad got out of the Brown Bomber.

I pretended I was holding a bugle and started playing that "Day Is Done . . ." song that they play at funerals.

"Byron, why won't you behave? Why won't you think about what's going to happen to you when you do something wrong? Why do you always do stuff to get people mad at you?" Joey asked.

"Why don't you make a break for it, Five Forty-one?" I asked.

We listened to the noises of Dad coming home from work, the *clump-clump* of his boots coming off and being dropped in the closet by the front door, the *whoosh* his chair made when he sat in it, Dad saying, "Whew, it sure is good to be home," the second *whoosh* of the chair when Momma sat in his lap, the sounds of kisses and giggles and laughs, then the words we'd waited for from Dad: "So what's new on the home front, Mrs. Watson?"

"Oh, not much. There is a surprise that one of your little darlings has for you, though."

"Good or bad?"

"Hmmm, well, I guess that depends on your point of view."

"Let me guess, which one of the crumb-crushers is going to surprise Big Daddy today?"

"Your first one."

"Oh Lord, what'd he do? How serious this time? It can't be too bad, you seem pretty calm."

"Well, let's just say I'm numb."

"That bad?"

"It depends. If you were happy with your son the way he was, this might be pretty bad. However, if you've always wanted a child from south of the border, you might be happy with the new young Mr. Watson."

"O.K., what's up?"

"Let me put it this way, do you remember the line Big Daddy used to give every girl at Central High School?"

"Hmmm, can't say I do."

"It goes like this: 'I can show you better than I can tell you.' Ring any bells?"

"Oh yeah, that does seem kind of familiar. Well, now's as good a time as any. Show me."

"All right, you asked for it. Byron dear, could you please come down here for a minute?" Momma didn't even raise her voice, she knew we'd been listening to everything they were saying.

Byron took a deep breath, then jumped off the top bunk and started down the stairs. I followed right behind him pretending I was a reporter. I shoved an imaginary microphone in his face.

"Any famous last words, Five Forty-one? Anything to say to all the little Chihuahuas before they start coming out of the woodwork? Do you think the governor might call before they pull the switch? Are you going to come clean and tell what led you down the road to crime?"

By figured he didn't have anything to lose so when we got about halfway down the steps he popped me square in the ear. Hard!

Getting hit when you're not expecting it can really shake you up. My legs started wobbling like my knees were made out of Jell-O, my eyes started leaking water, my nose started running.

I tried to go tell on By, but all I could do was sit on the next-to-the-last step and hold my ear as tears jumped out of my eyes. My throat wouldn't quit jerking up and down and making weird noises.

Joey sat on the step next to me with tears jumping out of her eyes too.

When Byron walked into the living room Momma said, "Mr. Watson, I'd like to introduce you to your long-lost son from Mexico City, Señor Byroncito Watson!"

Joey made me quit sobbing so we could see what Dad was going to do, but for the longest time there were no sounds from the living room.

We looked at each other.

Finally the chair whooshed as Momma got off of Dad's lap, then whooshed again as Dad stood up.

After a long time Dad said, "Uh, uh, uh."

Then, "Well, son, what can I say? It's pretty much permanent, isn't it." Dad's voice was real calm and that was scarier than if he'd been yelling.

"Yes, Dad."

"'Yes, Dad.' So there's really nothing I can do, is there."

"I don't think so, Dad."

"You don't think so, Dad. Well, judging by the condition of your hair I wouldn't say thinking is one of your strong suits, is it."

Byron mumbled something. Wow! He must have really felt like he didn't have anything to lose, 'cause Momma and Dad just didn't tolerate mumbling.

Dad's voice shifted. "Excuse me?"

"I said, 'No, Dad.'"

"'No, Dad.'"

Joey started boo-hooing again. Whenever Dad repeated everything you said like this some real big trouble was about to follow.

"Hmmm, you know, maybe there is something that can be done about this after all."

Suddenly Dad and Byron were in the doorway leading upstairs.

Dad looked surprised to see me and Joey sitting there. He smiled at us.

"Hi, Kenneth. Hi, Punkin. Why are you two crying?"

I could just point at my ear but Joey said, "Oh, Daddy, please, what are you gonna do?"

"Don't worry, Jo, everything's O.K., you just wait down here."

Dad and Byron disappeared into the bathroom and the door locked behind them.

Dad hadn't told me to wait downstairs so I ran up and stood at the bathroom door peeking through the keyhole. Someone had stuffed some toilet paper in the hole, though, so I had to drop to the floor and peek under the door to see what was going on.

From the way Dad and By's feet were standing I could tell that By was sitting on the toilet and Dad was standing at the sink.

Dad was rumbling around in the medicine cabinet.

I could hear By sniff a couple of times, then Dad started whistling that stupid song "Straighten Up and Fly Right."

Dad's feet took the two steps from the sink to the toilet.

Byron said, "Awww, man!" I heard a *choo-chicka* sound and the floor around their feet started being covered with stiff, reddish brown Mexican-style hair.

Dad kept whistling and cutting.

Choo-chicka.

"Awww, man."

"Hold your head still, I'd hate to take one of these ears off by mistake." Dad went on whistling.

Choo-chicka.

"Aww, man."

"Kenneth, what are you doing?" Momma called me from downstairs.

I ran from the door and got halfway down the steps before I said, "Nothing, Momma."

"Come on down *here* and do nothing."

"Yes, Momma."

"What's your father doing?"

"He's whistling 'Straighten Up and Fly Right' and cutting all of Byron's hair off!"

Momma laughed. Joey sat next to her still looking worried.

The three of us sat on the couch for about half an hour before we heard By scream as loud as he could.

Dad hollered down to us, "Just a little aftershave."

We heard the bathroom door open. Dad came down the steps first. "Mrs. Watson," he said, "I'd like to introduce you to your long-lost son from Siam, His Royal Highness, Yul Watson!"

Byron stepped into the living room with a real mean scowl on his face. Not only had Dad cut all of Byron's hair off, he'd also shaved his head! By's head was so shiny it looked like it was wet.

"And, Mrs. Watson," Dad said, "you can't possibly deny this is your child. You can tell this boy has got a ton of Sands blood in him, look at those ears!"

Poor Byron. If he'd have known how far his ears stuck out to the side I bet he never would have gotten that butter!

Momma put her hand over her mouth and said, "Lord, don't blame that on my side of the family, someone switched this child at the hospital!"

Joey laughed because she was relieved Byron hadn't been executed, Momma and Dad laughed at Byron's ears, but none of them laughed as hard as me.

"Go get the broom and dustpan and sweep that garbage in the bathroom up, then go stay in your room. This is it, By. You're old enough now and you've been told enough, this time something's going to be done. Now beat it." Dad's forehead was all wrinkled when he said this.

They sent me and Joey outside so they could have one of those adults-only talks.

When me and Joey drifted back into the house after what seemed enough time for them to talk, Dad was on the telephone. He was holding the receiver away from his ear and making a funny face.

I could hear someone yelling from the phone.

Dad whispered to Momma, "Why does she think she's got to yell into the phone for a long-distance call?"

Momma slapped his arm and whispered back, "You leave my momma alone!"

They were talking to Grandma Sands! All the way in Alabama!

Me and Joey crowded up next to them on the couch and heard Grandma Sands yell, "This is costing y'all a fortune, Daniel, let me talk to my baby again."

Dad handed the phone back to Momma, then dug his finger around in his ear like he was going deaf.

Momma gave Dad a dirty look and said, "O.K., Momma, we'll be getting back with you. We love you. Bye-bye." She said this stuff Southern-style.

And that was it. We thought that was the end of Byron's Latest Adventure until a week later when Dad brought home the TT AB-700 in the Brown Bomber.

8. The Ultra–Glide!

I don't know why we didn't catch on that something different was really going to happen this time, Momma and Dad started acting real strange right after they talked to Grandma Sands.

First Momma started writing in a notebook and adding things up and subtracting things, then Dad and Joey and Rufus and me started driving all over Flint buying things for the Brown Bomber.

We stopped at Genesee Junkyard and bought a new antenna for the radio and four new used tires, then we stopped at Mr. Biller's Garage and had the tires put on the car, then we stopped at the Yankee Store and bought some spark plugs and some oil and antifreeze, then we got our next-door neighbor Mr. Johnson to help put all that stuff in the car, then we washed and waxed the Brown Bomber.

When Byron walked by while we were working on it he said, "Y'all done real good. It still looks like a turd on wheels, but I gotta admit, now it looks like a polished turd."

We ignored him.

While Joey cleaned the windows, me and Rufus washed the seats, even the parts that were torn and worn away. But the more we washed them the worse they looked and Dad ended up going back to the Yankee Store and buying some brown-and-white seat covers for the front seat.

The Brown Bomber looked great! Not almost new, but not almost fifteen years old either. We brought Momma out and showed it to her and she gave us one of those big hand-over-her-mouth smiles.

"Well, folks," Dad said, and we all knew he was getting ready to cut up, "all it needs now is that final touch, that special something that sets it apart from all of the other buckets of bolts on the road, that one piece of all-American engineering that shows that this fine automobile is worthy of the name Brown Bomber. Any guesses as to what that is?"

"A new hood thing?" I asked. The thing in the middle of the hood was a long chrome rocket that pointed out over the road. The only thing that was wrong with it was that one of the wings of the rocket was broken off.

Like with everything else, Dad had a crazy explanation for that. He told us that right after he got the car from Uncle Bud both wings were there but that he had taken it to a special garage and had one wing "scientifically and mathematically" taken off.

When we asked him why, he told us that that way when we came back from a long trip we'd be "coming in on a wing and a prayer." That's the kind of junk Dad thinks is funny.

"No," Dad answered my question, "it's not a new hood thing. The one on there now is perfectly fine.

"Joey, what's your guess?"

"I don't know, Daddy, I don't think anything can make the Bomber any better, I think it's perfect."

"Bless you, sweetheart. Rufus, your turn, what do you think?"

"I don't know, Mr. Watson, I like y'all's car just fine."

"I knew there was something I liked about that boy. All right, Wilona, what's your guess?"

"I don't know either," Momma said, and rolled her eyes. "I think the car is per . . . per . . . per . . ." Momma was cutting up too. ". . . Oh my God, I can't say it!"

"Real cute, Wilona. Well, since Kenneth and Momma have insulted the Great Brown One, I guess that leaves it up to Rufus and Punkin to put the final piece on." Dad handed the keys to Rufus. "Rufus, you open the trunk, and Punkin, there's a small bag in there. You have the honor of putting what's inside of it on."

Rufus popped the trunk open and Joey took a small paper bag out. She turned her back to everyone and looked inside.

"Oh, Daddy, I love it!"

"Do you know where it goes?"

"Yes, Daddy."

"O.K., time's a-wasting, put it on."

She put her hand in the bag and, without pulling it out, said, "And now, the thing that makes this car more perfect . . ."

Dad started helping Joey cut up. He said, "The final touch."

Joey repeated, "The final touch!"

"The height of technology."

"The height of technology!"

"The ultimate in American knowledge."

"The ultimate in American knowledge!"

Momma couldn't take any more. "For God's sake, Daniel, what is it?"

"It's the pinnacle of Western civilization."

"It's the pea knuckle of Western civilization!"

"Now, Joey, dazzle 'em, girl!"

Joey pulled her hand out of the bag and said, "It's a smelly green pine tree!"

Momma went *"Ugh!"* and walked back into the house.

Joey hung the smelly green pine tree from the rearview mirror and scooted out of the car to let me and Rufus smell her fingers.

But Dad wasn't through adding things to the Brown Bomber. On Saturday morning Joey and me got up real early to watch cartoons and Dad was already up brushing his teeth and shaving. I went into the bathroom to watch him. I love the way that shaving soap smells.

"Hi, Dad."

"Morning, Kenny, how'd you sleep?" Dad said this with his toothbrush in his mouth.

"O.K., I guess."

Then Dad pulled one of his famous tricks on me. He said, "Kenny, look!" and pointed out in the hallway. Even before I could think my head turned around and I followed Dad's finger. When I saw nothing and looked back Dad was smiling a mile a minute, acting like he hadn't done anything but I noticed that his toothbrush was gone. I let him know he didn't fool me. "Dad, how come you always hide your toothbrush, why don't you keep yours with ours?"

Dad laughed. "Well, Kenny, I guess I don't keep my toothbrush with the rest of yours because unlike your mother, I was a little boy once myself."

I thought about this for a second, then said, "What does that mean?"

Dad picked up my toothbrush and said, "Look at this, not only is this instrument perfect for brushing teeth, it has other wonderful uses too. You see, Kenny, I know that in a little boy's eyes there isn't anything in the world that is better for general cleaning than a toothbrush, and the greatest thing about it is that with a good rinse afterward no one can tell what it was used for.

"I also know that the best toothbrush for cleaning stuff is always someone else's. So, rather than wondering what my toothbrush last cleaned, I think it's better that it only goes places that I know about."

Dad was right. I caught Byron using mine once to

shine up some quarters and another time to brush Blackie's teeth. I didn't really care but Blackie didn't like it. That was the only time he ever growled at someone in his own family.

Dad was stirring the soap dish up with his shaving brush, and I got close to the sink to smell the soap. Dad painted his face with the soap, then bent down and rinsed it off. I know it sounds crazy, but he always did this twice, he said it really made your beard super-soft. He learned that 'cause he used to work in a barbershop when he was a little boy. That's where he also learned that if you go to the barbershop you've got to make sure your neck is real clean, otherwise the barber talks about you like a dog after you leave.

"So," Dad said as he put the second coat of soap on his face, "let me guess why you're standing so close. Could it be that you want me to soap your face up and hold you up here while you shave it off? It's been a long time since we've done that."

"Aww, man, I'm way too old for that. Besides, I'm starting to get a real mustache. Look." I stuck my upper lip out for Dad to see.

"Where?" Dad leaned down and looked real hard. "I can't see it."

"Here, look."

"Maybe if you got closer to the light." Dad bent over and picked me up to the mirror. I automatically turned my head sideways when I saw my reflection. Some of the time I forgot all about my lazy eye.

"Well, I don't believe it! If you squint your eyes and look real hard, there's no doubt about it, this boy's got a real mustache going here!"

I didn't know if Dad really could see it or not, but I knew it was there. He put me down.

"Won't be long before you and I have to share the mirror in the morning, huh?"

I couldn't help it. Even though I knew he might be kidding, I broke out in a real big smile and nodded my head up and down.

Dad started shaving. "Well, just so there're no problems, I've got seniority on you, so I get the bathroom first, deal?"

"Deal!"

When Dad finished he asked me, "You too old for a little Old Spice?"

He slapped the cologne on me and said, "I don't want your mother to know I put this aftershave on you. What with you smelling so good and this new mustache coming out I don't want her blaming me when all these little girls start attacking you." I twisted my face up.

We walked into the living room to watch cartoons, but when we got there Dad kept going and said, "If your mother gets up before I'm back just tell her I won't be long."

"Where you going, Daddy?" Joey asked.

Dad gave his famous answer, "Out," and closed the door behind him.

Dad missed *Felix the Cat*, *Soupy Sales*, *Beany and Cecil*, *The Rae Deane Show* and *Betty Boop*. He missed

Momma getting up and Byron getting up. When he finally got back we were all sitting on the couch watching the worst cartoon ever made, *Clutch Cargo*.

Dad walked in and turned the TV off.

"Dad!"

"Sorry, kids, everybody's got to come outside right now. You too, Daddy-o, and you too, Wilona. I've got a surprise."

Dad made us stop at the front door and get in a line, one behind the other, Momma first, then Byron, then me, then Joey. Except for bald-headed By, we were all laughing and wondering what Dad's surprise was when he opened the door.

Following Dad, we walked down the front porch steps and stood on the sidewalk like a little parade. I bet the neighbors wondered what the Weird Watsons were doing this time.

"All right," Dad said, "when I say it, I want everybody to close their eyes, and I'm warning you, anyone who looks before I tell you to is going to get it."

My eyes, of course, would be sealed. If a bomb exploded under me I'd be standing in the hole with my eyes sealed. Even if my head got blown off they'd have to say, "Here's that kid's head, and yup, his eyes are locked tight as a safe!"

Byron said I was stupid for listening to everything that Momma and Dad said, but if I was so stupid why was he the one who had a great big, bald, shiny, knotted-up head?

Dad said, "O.K., now hold the person in front of you

by the shoulders. Wilona, you hold on to mine. This is only going to take a minute."

He said that last part because Momma rolled her eyes and was real close to stopping everything by turning around and going back into the house.

"All right, close 'em."

Momma gave him her "last straw" look and closed her eyes, then so did we. Dad shuffled us ahead a little bit and then we all stopped. It was real hard not to peek.

"O.K., keep 'em shut, I'm not playing."

I heard a car door open, heard a loud pop, then heard Byron say, "Awww, man . . ."

Me and Joey cracked up. We knew a certain person had peeked and got popped, right smack-jab on that bald head.

Finally Dad said, "That's it, open your eyes. What do you think?"

Dad had opened the driver's side of the Brown Bomber and was standing with one arm pointing the way inside.

In the middle of the dashboard, to the right of the steering wheel, something real big was sticking out. Dad had taken one of our giant towels and set it over the thing. Everybody stood there staring.

Finally Momma said, "Daniel, what on earth is that towel doing in there?"

"The towel is fine, Wilona. Aren't you wondering what's underneath it?"

"Yeah, Dad, what is that thing?" I asked.

"Well, Kenneth, since you seem to be the only one with any curiosity, I guess you'll be the one who gets to unveil the Bomber's latest addition."

I crawled into the front seat and raised a corner of the towel so no one but me could see what was under it. I couldn't believe it!

"Dad, it's great!"

The rest of them, Byron included, crowded up to the Brown Bomber's door.

Momma had a worried voice. "What have you done to this car now? Daniel, what's under that towel?"

I grabbed a corner of the towel. "Ladies and gentle—"

Byron interrupted me when he saw I was going to tease them. He said, "Awww, man, just pull the blanged towel off so I can get outta here. I ain't got all day to listen to your mess." He was always in a hurry to get out of someplace but never had anywhere else to go.

"Byron, how many times have I told you about saying 'ain't,' and Kenneth, you stop playing and move that towel this minute!" Momma said.

I talked real fast before Momma could get any madder. "Ladies and gentlemen, the newest addition to the Brown Bomber!" I whipped the towel aside. "Our very own drive-around record player!"

Momma went, "Oh my God!" and gave Dad a dirty look, then walked back into the house.

Joey squealed, "Oh boy!"

Even cool old Byron forgot how cool he was and

screamed out, "Awww, man, this is too, too hip! No one's got one of these. Speedy don't even have one in his Cadillac! Too much, man, way too much!"

Joey and Byron climbed into the car on either side of me.

We all said, "Turn it on, Daddy!"

I knew Dad was kind of disappointed by the way Momma had acted. She really hurt his feelings by walking off like that. Some of the time I think she forgot how sensitive Dad was. Even though he acted cheery with us I knew it wasn't the same for him now. I knew if Momma had stayed and hadn't gone off mumbling about money we would have been having a lot more fun.

But Dad forgot all this stuff real quick and got excited about showing off the record player. Dad was like me, he loved putting on a show, or as Momma said, we both loved acting the fool. Dad was the best at it, though, and I couldn't wait until I was as good as he was.

"Well, well, well," Dad said, leaning down into the car, "I see you three have the ultimate in taste. I see you've chosen the top of the line, the cream of the crop, the True-Tone AB-700 model, the Ultra-Glide!"

We had too, 'cause right on the front of the record player in big red letters it said, "TT AB-700, Ultra-Glide"!

"As I'm certain you are aware, the problem in the past with this new technology in automotive sound has been road vibrations interfering with an accurate dispersal of the phonic interpretations."

"Huh?" Byron said.

Dad said, "In other words, I'm sure you know that in the good old days every time you drove over a bump with one of these things the needle would jump and scratch the record."

Me and Joey played along. "We know, we know!"

"And, as I'm sure such a fine, intelligent-looking family as this one . . . it *is* Mr. and Mrs. Watson and your son, isn't it?"

"Oh no," Joetta said, and pointed at Byron. "This isn't our son, this is just a little juvenile delinquent boy that we feel sorry for and let follow us around some of the time. Our real son has hair!"

Even this didn't bother Byron, who was amazed by the Brown Bomber's latest addition.

Dad kept imitating the guy who sold him the record player. "Yes, as I'm sure a nice family like this one is aware, it was only last year that the scientists at Autotronic Industries made a brilliant, beautiful, breathtaking breakthrough and developed a suitable system for controlling these vibrations."

"Yeah," I said, "I saw it last night on the news. Walter Cronkite said it was a miracle!"

Dad laughed. "Precisely, Mr. Watson. Walt has two of these babies in his car and one on his motorcycle!"

"We know, we know!"

"Yes, the vibration problem has been overcome by the exclusive Vibro-Dynamic-Lateral-Anti-Inertial Dampening system."

Dad had memorized that word 'cause right on the

arm of the record player it said "V.D.L.A.I. Dampening, Patented"!

"Come on, Daddy, turn it on, stop teasing!"

"Now, now, Mrs. Watson, be patient, and tell that little-delinquent-that-follows-you-around that if he touches one more knob on that record player I am going to pull his fingers off"

Byron mumbled and sat back in the seat.

"Before I dazzle you with the symphonic sound of this unit, let me point out some of its less-appreciated features."

"Oh, please do."

"Awww, man, just turn the blanged thing on. If I gotta listen to all this jive I'm gonna go in the house and get some *real* cool sounds." Byron opened the passenger door and ran into the house.

"Now, Mr. and Mrs. Watson, I'd like to direct your attention to the rear of your classic automobile."

Me and Joey crawled up on the backseat and looked at the back window. On the rear shelf a hole had been cut and was covered with that same stuff that's on a screen door.

"I can see you're wondering what that is. Well, let me explain. What we have here is, believe it or not, a second speaker! And I can tell by that intelligent look on your face, Mrs. Watson, that you have grasped that that speaker is not placed in the rear deck haphazardly, no, ma'am.

"Some people think we just have a hole hacked in back there by any old mechanic, but nothing could be further from the truth. That opening is scientifically and mathematically positioned by a factory-trained technician to enhance the TT AB-700's true high-fidelity sound!"

"Wow!"

Byron exploded through the front door with an armful of 45s and Momma right on his tail.

"Byron Watson, don't you stomp on those stairs like that and don't you slam that screen door!"

She trailed Byron all the way to the car, fussing at him the whole way. I knew she was using Byron as an excuse to come back out and see what was going on. I guess all the laughing and fun we were having made her want to join in.

Now that she was back Dad started really cutting up.

"Well, well, well, Mrs. Watson," Dad said, but not to Momma, to Joey, "I see your beautiful young daughter has decided to join us, and not a moment too soon either. Why don't you scoot over a bit and let her in."

Joey loved this chance to pretend she was Momma's mom. She patted the seat next to her and said, "Come on in, honey, this is really cool!"

Momma slid in under the steering wheel with a halfway smile on her face.

"Wunnerful, wunnerful!" Dad said.

Byron lifted the record that was already on the turntable and started putting one of his own cool songs on.

"Put it back, son, you'll get your turn. First we have a special request from a certain young lady to a certain handsome young man. If you'll excuse me, ma'am, I'll just reach over here and get this show on the road." Dad reached over past Momma to start the car, but on the way his hand kind of accidentally on purpose brushed her chests.

Boy, did they think we were blind? Even though Dad thought he was being slick, everybody saw this.

Momma puckered up her lips to squeeze down a smile and crossed her arms over her chests, Joetta giggled and me and Byron scrunched our faces up.

Momma did a fakety little slap at his hand and smiled.

Dad turned the key and the Brown Bomber fired up.

"O.K., young lady, here's that special number you requested."

Dad couldn't help himself and started imitating a disc jockey.

"Here's the man with the patter,
Here to spin the platter,
Why, it doesn't matter,
'Cause the world is getting fatter.
I'm the man with the tune
That'll take you to the moon,
That'll make your poor heart swoon,
I'll hold you like a spoon.
I'm the man with the jive . . ."

Byron chirped up, "Ain't that the whole natural truth?" but Dad didn't miss a beat.

". . . Put your love thing in drive,
Bring your little world alive . . ."

Momma slapped the car seat. "Daniel, start that record!"

"All right, all right." Dad stopped his rhyming, not because Momma told him to, but because I bet he ran out of stupid poems.

"But first, let me tell all you people out there in Radio-Land that this number was requested by a Miss Wilona Sands for the wunnerful, wunnerful man in her life, the Big Daddy of love, Daniel Watson. We at Flint's only soul station, WAMM, dedicate this song to Daniel, from Wilona. Spin it, maestro!"

Dad reached over past Momma to start the record player.

Joey grabbed my arm with one hand and squealed into her other one.

Byron was grinning like a giant, bald-headed kindergarten baby.

Momma still had her arms crossed but was starting to smile. She brought one hand up to cover her mouth.

My foot was tapping on the Brown Bomber's floor a mile a minute and I couldn't make it stop no matter what I did. I guess I was grinning pretty hard too.

Dad's hand touched a knob that had "Start" written on it, but before he turned it he pulled his hand back and said, "First, however . . ."

We all screamed.

"Daddy!"

"Awww, man!"

"Come on, Dad!"

"Daniel!"

But Dad wasn't through yet, and you couldn't rush him. In fact, the more you'd complain, the longer he'd take.

He put his hand up to stop the noise. "But, first, we at WAMM want to apologize to the nine other women who called in requesting love songs to be dedicated to Daniel Watson. If they stay tuned, we'll play their songs later in the evening."

Momma said, "That's it," and started climbing out of the car. It was a fun "That's it," though, not a serious one.

Dad blocked the door and finally, finally turned the knob that said "Start." Then he got into the backseat.

We all froze. Even the Brown Bomber seemed to get quieter as the V.D.L.A.I. arm from the record player lifted itself and moved toward the 45 that was on the turntable. The arm dropped and a hollow little boom bounced around in the car. A moment of silence and then . . .

And then the most beautiful notes of music I'd ever heard came from the front of the car and the back of the car at the same time.

> "DOOM, DA-DOOM DOOM,
> DOOM, DA-DOOM DOOM,
> DOOM, DA-DOOM DOOM,
> DOOM!"

The notes were so deep and strong it felt like we were sitting inside a giant bass fiddle.

Momma screamed and put both of her hands over her mouth. She'd recognized "her song" after the first couple of notes.

The guy on the record started singing "Under the Boardwalk" and I had to turn around and look because it sounded like he was right in the backseat with Dad.

We sat in the car for almost two hours as everybody got a chance to go in the house and get their favorite records.

Even though we had a pretty good record player in the house, it couldn't compare with the sounds that came from the scientifically and mathematically put-in speakers that the Brown Bomber had. The Ultra-Glide cast a spell on all of the Weird Watsons.

Byron was always saying that Momma couldn't stand to see anyone having too much fun; but, to be fair to her, I have to say that she stopped us from having fun in steps instead of doing it all at once.

First she thought the music was too loud and made us turn it down some; then after all of us kids got to play four songs each (I played "Yakety Yak" all four of my times) she made us get out of the car and she and Dad played Nat King Cole and Dinah Washington and other mush-ball singers; then she said to Dad, "Did you tell them yet?"

Oh-oh! I leaned into the car to get a look at Momma's stomach. This sounded like the way Byron and me found out we were going to get a sister.

Everybody's ears jumped up. Something big was going on.

Dad wasn't too comfortable with things like this and said, "No, it can wait."

"No, it can't."

Momma let the last song finish, then said, "Turn it off, Daniel.

"Children, in a little bit Daddy's going to get some vacation time and we're going to drive to Alabama. Grandma Sands is going to keep Byron for the summer and if things don't work out he'll stay there for the next school year."

This was too good to be true, a long trip in the Brown Bomber and no Byron for the whole summer! And probably for the whole year, 'cause when it came to Byron nothing *ever* worked out!

Byron looked at Momma and Dad with his mouth wide open.

"We've been telling you, Byron, you've been given warning after warning and chance after chance to straighten up, but instead of improving, you're getting worse. Do I have to remind you of the things you've done just this last year?"

Byron still didn't close his mouth.

Momma started ticking off the things that Byron called his Latest Fantastic Adventures.

"You've cut school so much that Mr. Alums has come here three times to see what's wrong with you, you've been lighting fires, you've been taking change out of my purse, you've been in fights, you had that trouble up at Mitchell's Food Fair, you had that . . . that . . . problem with Mary Ann Hill, you set mousetraps in the backyard for birds, you fell out of that tree when you were trying to see if that poor cat always landed on its feet, you got that conk, you joined that gang. . . . There's just too much, Byron. We can't have all this nonsense going on."

I hoped those weren't the only Latest Fantastic Adventures that Momma knew about. I could list about a hundred more.

"That's why Grandma Sands is going to look after you for a while. You're about to run us crazy."

Momma changed the tone of her voice. "You're going to like Birmingham, Byron. It's a lot different than Flint. There are lots of nice boys your age down there who you can be friends with. There's lots of fishing and hunting that you can do. Things are a lot better there. I love that city. Your grandma tells me it's quiet in our old neighborhood, she says that that stuff on TV isn't happening around her. It's just like I remember it being, it's safe, it's quiet. And there's no Buphead!"

Momma and Dad had threatened to send Byron to Grandma Sands about a million times but we never thought it would happen. This was for three good reasons.

The first reason was that Alabama was about two million miles from Flint and By knew Momma wouldn't let him ride the bus that far alone. He also knew it would be just about impossible for her to sit on a bus with him for the three days it took to get there.

The second reason was that Momma and Dad were always threatening to do stuff to Byron that everybody knew they wouldn't do. Dad had been keeping a count-down on how many more months it would be before they could force him to join the army, but we knew they wouldn't do that.

But the biggest reason Byron and Joey and me thought they'd never send him to Alabama was because we had heard so many horrible stories about how strict Grandma Sands was. The thought of living with her was so terrible that your brain would throw it out as soon as it came in.

Well, Byron's brain had better get used to it, we all knew by the way they'd gotten the Bomber ready and by the way Momma's voice sounded that they meant it this time.

The big, cool baby finally shut his mouth and ran into the house. He slammed the door as hard as he could and we all heard him say, real clear, the *S* word.

Joey said, "Oooh . . ."

Dad started to go in after him but Momma said, "Let him go, Daniel, he better get as much of that nonsense out of his system as he can. Grandma Sands won't be putting up with any of that mess."

9. The Watsons Go to Birmingham—1963

That Sunday I got up early. There weren't any cartoons on then but it was always fun to wake up and not have to worry about going to school.

When I got into the living room I was surprised to see the front door open. I looked outside and saw Dad sitting in the Brown Bomber. I guess he was listening to records because he had his arm across the seat and was beating his hand up and down like it was a drum.

I ran back upstairs to the bedroom and changed out of my pajamas. I peeked out of the bedroom window to make sure Dad hadn't left. He was still in the car so I ran downstairs and through the front door. I remembered and caught the screen just before it slammed.

I tapped on the window and Dad turned and smiled at me, then pointed to the passenger side for me to get in. I ran around the car and climbed in.

"Hey, Kenny."

"Hi, Dad."

"How'd you sleep?"

"O.K., I guess."

"Go on in and get 'Yakety Yak' and sit with me for a while."

"That's O.K., I'll just listen to what you're playing."

We listened to a couple of jive songs and then I said, "Dad, does Byron really have to go to Alabama? Couldn't we just drive down to about Ohio and pretend we're going to leave him to scare him?"

Dad looked at me and smiled kind of slow. He reached over and turned the Ultra-Glide down a little bit. "Kenneth, I know you're going to miss Byron, we all will, but son, there are some things that Byron has to learn and he's not learning them in Flint, and the things he is learning are things we don't want him to. Do you understand?"

"No."

Dad turned the Ultra-Glide down a little more. He looked like he was thinking whether or not he should tell me something. He was looking straight at me, and even though it was real hard, I looked right back at him.

I tried to look real intelligent and I guess it worked 'cause finally Dad said, "Kenny, we've put a lot of thought into this. I know you've seen on the news what's happening in some parts of the South, right?"

We'd seen the pictures of a bunch of really mad white people with twisted-up faces screaming and giving dirty finger signs to some little Negro kids who were trying to go to school. I'd seen the pictures but I didn't really know how these white people could hate some kids so much.

"I've seen it." I didn't have to tell Dad I didn't understand.

"Well, a lot of times that's going to be the way of the world for you kids. Byron is getting old enough to have to understand that his time for playing is running out fast, he's got to realize the world doesn't have a lot of jokes waiting for him. He's got to be ready."

Dad looked at me again to make sure I was understanding. I nodded.

"Grandma Sands says it's quiet down where they are, but we think it's time Byron got an idea of the kind of place the world can be, and maybe spending some time down South will help open his eyes."

I nodded my head again.

"Momma and I are very worried because there're so many things that can go wrong to a young person and Byron seems bound and determined to find every one of them.

"Now, do you really understand why we're sending Byron to Birmingham?"

"I think so, Dad."

"Good, because, Kenny, we've done all we can and it seems the temptations are just too much for By here in Flint. So hopefully, the slower pace in Alabama will help him by removing some of those temptations. Hopefully he can see that there comes a time to let all of the silliness go. By'll be back, maybe at the end of the summer, maybe next year. It's completely in his own hands now."

I loved when Dad talked to me like I was grown-up. I didn't really understand half the junk he was saying, but it sure did feel good to be talked to like that!

It's times like this when someone is talking to you like you are a grown-up that you have to be careful not to pick your nose or dig your drawers out of your butt.

"O.K., Dad, thanks." He smiled again, turned the Ultra-Glide back up and ran his hand over my head.

Some of the time when you think about being a grown-up it gets to be kind of scary. I couldn't figure out how Momma and Dad knew how to take care of things. I couldn't figure out how they knew what to do with Byron.

"Dad?"

"Hmmm?"

"I don't think I'll ever know what to do when I'm a grown-up. It seems like you and Momma know a lot of things that I can never learn. It seems real scary. I don't think I could ever be as good a parent as you guys."

Dad turned the Ultra-Glide back down. "Kenny, do you remember when we used to go on drives and I'd put you in my lap and let you steer the car?"

I smiled. "Yeah, does that mean I get to do it on the way to Alabama?"

"Sure, but that's not what I meant. Do you remember how big and scary the car seemed to be the first time you were behind the wheel?"

Dad was right. Even though I knew he was watching

everything real close it still was scary to steer the Brown Bomber.

"Well, that's what being a grown-up is like. At first it's scary but then before you realize, with a lot of practice, you have it under control. Hopefully you'll have lots of time to practice being grown-up before you actually have to do it."

This was making sense to me.

"And as far as you being a good parent, don't worry. You'll learn from the mistakes your mother and I make, just like we learned from the mistakes our parents made. I don't have a single doubt that you and Byron and Joey will be much better parents than your mother and I ever were." Dad stopped talking for a second. "Besides, some of the time we don't think we've done such a good job. But you're right, Kenneth, it can be scary, and it gets a lot scarier when you see you're responsible for three little lives. A lot scarier."

I waited to see if Dad was going to talk to me like this anymore but he turned the music back up. We listened to his junk a little more, and then I said, "Dad?"

"Yeah."

"I've got one more question."

He turned the Ultra-Glide down a little again and gave me his serious look. "What do you want to know, Kenny?"

"Is it too late to go get 'Yakety Yak'?"

Dad laughed and sent me in to get it. I had to promise to play it only three times, though.

After the third time I asked, "Dad, why did you buy

this record player? Don't they have radio stations in Ala-bama?"

"Sure they do, lots of them, but you see, once you get south of Cincinnati the only kind of radio station you can get is hillbilly music. And you won't believe this, but if you listen to any kind of music long enough, first you get accustomed to it and then you learn to like it.

"Now, your mother and I made a deal when we first got married that if either one of us ever watched the 'wunnerful, wunnerful' *Lawrence Welk Show* or listened to country music the other one got to get a free divorce. I'm kind of used to your mother and I don't want to have her dump me, so instead of taking the chance I would get hooked on hillbilly music I thought it would be wise to bring our own sounds along with us."

Even though this made sense to me, Momma didn't buy it, and for the next week, while we were getting everything set for going to Alabama, she kept reminding Dad how much the Ultra-Glide cost and how it messed up all the plans she'd written in her notebook.

Me and Joey were in the living room playing when Momma and our neighbor Mrs. Davidson came in.

"Hello, Joetta. Hello, Kenneth."

"Hi, Mrs. Davidson."

I noticed right away that she had something behind her back. She said, "Since I won't be seeing you for a while I thought I'd give you something so you wouldn't forget about me, sweetheart." She stuck a box out toward Joey.

I could kill Joey the way she opened presents. Instead of ripping the wrapping paper off she hunted around to find each piece of tape, then peeled it off real careful. It took her about two days to get all the paper off and open the box. Joey finally held up her present.

I didn't think Mrs. Davidson noticed but I could tell there was something that Joey wasn't too happy about. She looked at Momma real quick and Momma looked at her, then Joey said, "Thank you very much, Mrs. Davidson."

Momma smiled.

Mrs. Davidson took the present from Joey and handed it to Momma. "See, Wilona, it's just like I told you. Look at that smile! The minute I saw it it reminded me of Joetta! Is that her smile or what? In fact, do you know what I named this angel?"

Joey pretended she was stupid and said, "No, Mrs. Davidson."

"I've named her after my favorite little girl, this angel's name is Joetta!"

I went over for a closer look. Mrs. Davidson had bought Joey a little angel that was kind of chubby and had big wings and a halo made out of straw. The only thing about its smile that looked like Joey to me was that the angel had a great big dimple too. It was made out of white clay and it looked like someone had forgotten to paint it. The only thing that had any color on it were its cheeks and its eyes. The cheeks were red and the eyes were blue.

Mrs. Davidson said, "Ooh, child, give me one more big hug before I go."

Joey got up and hugged Mrs. Davidson, then took her angel and said, "I'm going to put her in my room. Thank you, Mrs. Davidson."

"You're welcome, precious." Mrs. Davidson looked like she was going to cry. We all knew she'd kidnap Joey if she had the chance. She liked her that much.

When Mrs. Davidson left, Momma went upstairs and into Joey's room.

I eavesdropped.

They were both sitting on Joey's bed.

"I was very proud of the way you behaved, Joetta. What was wrong?"

"That angel, Mommy."

"Oh?"

"Mrs. Davidson said it reminded her of me, but it didn't look like me at all."

Momma looked around the room. "Where'd you put it?"

"It's in my socks drawer."

Joey was so neat she had a separate drawer for socks.

Momma went and got the angel and sat next to Joey.

"Sweetheart, I can see how it reminds her of you. Look at that dimple."

"But Mommy, it's white."

Momma laughed. "Well, honey, I can't say it isn't, but an angel's an angel, what do you think?"

"Maybe, but I know that angel's name isn't Joetta Watson."

"Well, I'm glad you didn't hurt Mrs. Davidson's feelings. Keep the angel around, you might get to like it. Where do you want me to put it?"

"Back under the socks."

Momma laughed.

The only one who didn't do anything to get ready to go to Alabama was Byron. He acted like nothing was going to happen, even though Momma got a bunch of our clothes together and put them in suitcases.

The smelly green pine tree was hung from the rearview mirror and all the lists and figuring were done, but Byron acted like he didn't notice. Even after a few more yelling phone calls were made to Alabama, Daddy Cool just kept being cool.

Byron didn't even get nervous when Momma packed a whole bunch of food in the giant green cooler we borrowed from the Johnsons. After all of this stuff it was finally the night before we were supposed to leave.

We'd just got in bed. Byron was up in his bunk and I was down in mine. I was so excited that I was talking a mile a minute, but I was talking to myself. Byron wouldn't answer or anything. There was a knock at our bedroom door.

"Come in."

It was Momma and Dad. Momma said, "Lights out, Kenneth. Byron, you come with us."

"What for?"

"We thought since this was the last night you were going to be spending in Flint for a while that you might like to sleep in our room tonight."

"You thought what?" Byron had a way of saying stuff in a few words that made it seem like he was saying a whole bunch more.

"Come on, By, you're bunking with us tonight," Dad said.

"Awww, man . . ."

Byron jumped out of the top bunk and gave me his Death Stare.

I just shrugged.

I guess the grapevine had gotten back to Momma and Dad that By was going to make a prison break tonight before he got transferred to Alabama. He thought I was the snitch but it was Joey.

She knew if Momma and Dad got up in the morning and Byron had flown the coop that he'd really be a dead man when they finally recaptured him, so I guess she saved his life by snitching. But By sure didn't appreciate it.

I sneaked out of bed after Momma and Dad arrested Byron. I was too excited to sleep and too excited to read. I looked out of the window at the Brown Bomber and couldn't believe it was going to take us all the way to Alabama.

The trip didn't become real to us until nine in the morning when we were in the car waving good-bye to

Rufus and heading toward I-75, a road that runs all the way from Flint to Florida. One road!

We weren't even on the expressway before Momma started reading out of her notebook telling us everything that was planned for the next three days.

"Day One, today. We leave Flint and drive for three hundred miles in about five or five and a half hours, that will take us to Cincinnati."

Three hundred miles in one day! It just didn't seem like that could be done. Me and Joey shook our heads. Byron looked out of the window.

"In Cincinnati we'll get a room in a motel. We brought plenty of blankets so you kids will be able to sleep on the floor."

Me and Joey cheered. We'd never been in a motel before. Byron just kept looking out of the window.

"Day Two, tomorrow. Now your Daddy and this car both aren't as young as they used to be so we don't want to push either one of them too hard." Dad looked shocked.

"So we rise and shine real early in the morning and drive for two hundred and fifty miles in about five or six hours. That should put us right outside of Knoxville, Tennessee. Mr. Johnson says that there are some clean, safe rest stops there so we can spend the night in the car. If that's true we'll stay there, if not we'll have to see if we can find a motel room in Knoxville.

"Day Three, Monday. This is going to be a tough day for your daddy because he's gonna have to drive for more than six hours. After we leave Knoxville we've got about three hundred miles to go. If we leave early enough we'll be pulling in to home about three in the afternoon." Momma turned the page in her notebook.

"We're gonna be able to stop once a day on the way down for hamburgers and once a day on the way back."

Me and Joey cheered again at this news. Byron acted like he didn't hear.

"Now, if we sleep in the car outside Knoxville we can stop one more bonus time coming and going, otherwise the cooler in the trunk is full of chicken, soda pop, potato salad, sandwiches and fruit for the whole trip down. I'm sure Grandma Sands will have everything set for the way back."

I thought about it for a minute, then asked, "Momma, how come we don't just drive until Dad gets tired, then stop?"

Dad did an imitation of a hillbilly accent. "'Cuz, boy, this he-uh is the deep South you-all is gonna be drivin' thoo. Y'all colored folks cain't be jes' pullin' up tuh any ol' way-uh an be 'spectin' tuh get no room uh no food, yuh heah, boy? I said yuh heah what I'm sayin', boy?"

Me and Joey laughed again, and even Byron kind of smiled. This only encouraged Dad to say some more Southern-style stuff.

"Y'all didn't know that, boy? Whas a mattah wit' choo, you thank this he-uh is Uhmurica?"

Momma had everything planned about the trip, everything! Where we'd eat, when we'd eat, who got baloney sandwiches on Day One, who got tuna fish on Day Two, who got peanut butter and jelly on Day Three. She'd figured out how long we could hold ourselves between going to the bathroom, how much money we'd spend on hamburgers, how much was for any emergencies, everything. She'd figured out who'd get the windows on each day and who was responsible for keeping paper and junk from piling up in the car.

When she finished reading all that stuff to us I asked her if I could look at the notebook. She handed it to me and I saw written on the cover in big, black letters, "The Watsons Go to Birmingham—1963." She'd even drawn a picture of a flower with a big, fat, stupid bird trying to land on it. Man, Momma sure is a bad artist!

"Why is this bird trying to land on a flower, Momma?"

Dad cracked up. "Ooh, Kenneth, I asked her the same thing and she was highly offended."

Momma said, "That's not a bird, that's a bee!"

I guess if you squinted up your eyes it might look like a bee, but not too much.

Momma'd also gone to the library to look up stuff about every state we'd travel through. We heard a bunch of boring junk about the expressway—how many years it took to finish it, how many miles long it was, how much it cost to build it, how it ran all the way from the Upper Peninsula in Michigan to Florida, all kinds of thrilling news. The only thing that was a little bit interesting was how many people got killed and hurt making the road. You never would think putting an expressway down was so dangerous.

She'd bought books and puzzles and games too. She really did try to make the trip interesting. The most interesting part for me, though, was going to be Byron.

Two days before we'd left, Buphead came by to visit Byron. The three of us were in my and By's bedroom. They'd tried to bully me out of the room but I stayed. They were sitting in the upper bunk and I was in the lower one.

"Man," Buphead complained, "I couldn't live with your ol' man, we'd be comin' to blows daily, Jack!"

"What can I say?" Byron answered.

"Not much. I can't believe they gonna make you spend the whole blanged summer in hot ol' Alabama. Shoot, I'd find somewhere else to stay. You gonna be black as the ace of spades when you get back, they got some sho-nuff sun down there!"

"Yeah, but dig, I got a way to pay them jive old squares back."

"Yeah, what you gonna do?"

"I ain't even sure I'm gonna go but if I do I know how they is, they gonna try some of that Ozzie and Harriet TV show mess on the way down, you know, playing games and counting cows and guessing how many red cars we gonna see in the next two miles and all that kind of three-six-nine, but I'm ready for 'em."

"Yeah?"

"Yeah, I got somethin' that'll mess that junk up for all of 'em!"

"What's that, Daddy-o?"

Byron remembered I was still in the lower bunk and stuck his head over the edge, then pointed at me. "You say one word about this to anyone and I'm gonna jack your little lightweight behind up, you hear?"

I said, "Awww, man . . .

By disappeared back into the top bunk. "Yeah, Buphead, if I do go I'm gonna go that whole blanged trip and, no matter what they do to me, I ain't gonna say one single word!"

"Whoa! How long that trip gonna take?"

"Three days."

"Cool, that'll show 'em."

They slapped palms and By said, "Yeah, you know it will."

But as soon as we got to Detroit, Byron said, "How we gonna work this record player?"

Dad looked in the rearview mirror and said to By, "What do you mean?"

"We gonna take turns?"

"Well, Byron, I don't think we'll be playing it for quite a bit yet, we can carry CKLW all the way down into Ohio and they play some pretty good music."

"But when we do play it, we gonna take turns?"

"Sure."

"Cool, am I first?"

"Sure, we'll go by seniority." Dad was in the United

Auto Workers at work so seniority was real important in our house.

"Cool."

I couldn't help myself, I leaned over Joey and said kind of quiet to By, "I guess you really showed them, didn't you? Boy, they were really begging you to talk, weren't they, Daddy-o?"

Byron made sure Joey wasn't watching, then flipped me a dirty finger sign and made his eyes go crossed.

"On the left, kids, is Tiger Stadium!" Momma was pointing out all the important things we passed on the way.

As the payback for giving me the dirty finger I said out loud to By, "How many cows you counted, By? How many red cars so far?"

He gave me his famous Death Stare, then leaned over Joey and whispered, "No cars, no cows, but I counted yo' momma six times already."

I couldn't believe it! What kind of person would talk about their own momma? I said, "That's *your* mother too, stupid!" I knew he didn't care, though. But I had to get him back, so I called him the only thing that bothered him. I said, "You might have counted my momma six times, but have you counted your mouth lately, Lipless Wonder?"

I got him! He showed his teeth and said, "You lit-tle . . ." and tried to grab me.

Dad's eye was in the rearview mirror.

"All right, you two, I said no nonsense and I don't mean maybe."

Byron used silent mouth language to say, "I'm gonna jack you up in Alabama, you punk!"

So as we drove down I-75 headed for Birmingham I felt pretty good. Even though every time I looked at By his eyes were crossed I didn't care because this one time I bugged him more than he bugged me!

10. Tangled Up in God's Beard

"Ohio, about one minute away!" This was the first interesting thing that Momma had come up with since we'd been through Detroit. Just outside of Toledo we pulled over at a rest stop.

Momma said, "O.K., who's got to go to the bathroom? Who's hungry?" We got out of the car and started scratching and stretching.

The Ohio rest stop was really cool! It was chopped right out of the forest and had picnic tables made out of giant logs. The bathrooms were made out of the same kind of log cabin wood. The only thing about them was that they looked kind of small from the outside.

Momma looked in her "Watsons Go to Birmingham —1963" book and told us, "O.K., just a sandwich, some fruit and some Kool-Aid here. Daniel, could you open the trunk so I can get the things out of the cooler?"

While Momma got the food and Dad looked under

the hood of the Brown Bomber I went to the door in the little log cabin that had "Men" carved on it.

As soon as I opened the door I gagged! The toilets in Ohio weren't anything like Michigan toilets. Instead of a white stool with a seat there was just a seat on a piece of wood with a great big, open, black hole underneath with the sound of flies coming out of it. No flusher, no water, no nothing. It looked like if you sat on the seat you might end up getting sucked down under Ohio somewhere!

I breathed through my mouth and spent only enough time in that log cabin bathroom to unroll a bunch of toilet paper. The woods outside looked like a whole lot better bathroom.

When I was done in the woods I passed Byron, who forgot again about his promise not to talk. He told me, "Man, they must be crazy if they think I'ma set my behind on that hole." By's hands were full of toilet paper too.

We ate our lunch on one of the picnic tables and Momma made a jug of Kool-Aid with water that me and Joey pumped. Only Momma liked it, though. The water seemed like it had metal in it and made the Kool-Aid taste like grape medicine.

Me, Dad, By and Joey dumped our Kool-Aid when Momma wasn't looking, but I had to ask for seconds and plug my nose and drink it because Day One was my day to have peanut butter and jelly and Momma always puts too much peanut butter on the sandwich and you've got to have something to wash it down in case you start choking.

When we finished eating Byron asked, "What's the word on them toilets?"

Momma and Dad cracked up.

"So you like those, huh?" Dad said.

Momma said, "You better get used to those, Byron, that's an outhouse and that's what Grandma Sands has."

"What?" If you try to be cool all the time and something surprises you you sure do look stupid.

"Uh-huh," Dad said, "that's where you're going to be taking care of your business for a while."

By said, "Wait, let me dig this, you mean if I gotta go to the bathroom I got to go outside into a little nasty thing like that? Ain't they got no sanitation laws down there? How you gonna have a hole for a toilet and not get folks sick? Don't them things attract flies?"

Momma and Dad laughed again. Momma said, "Your grandma Sands always says it seems a lot nastier to her to be doing that in the house. The way she looks at it a house is a whole lot nicer place if the facilities are outside."

"Ooh, I remember those outhouses!" Dad said. "I remember when we used to go visit my grandmother in the country and there would be a Sears catalog in the outhouse and when you were done you just tore a page out of the catalog and—"

"We get the point, Daniel." Momma stopped Dad. After lunch By went back into the log cabin outhouse and came back with his pockets bulging with toilet paper. He told me, "Man, they must be on dope if they think I'ma wipe my butt on some rough of catalog paper."

We loaded the cooler back in the car and got back on I-75.

When you're ten years old, like me, some of the time no matter how excited you are, or no matter how hard you try, you just can't help falling asleep in the car. I did a lot better than Joey, though. She was out before I'd even sucked all the leftover peanut butter out of my teeth.

She stretched out across the backseat and me and By argued about who would hold her head and who would hold her feet. Joey drooled a lot and so it was the worse job to hold her head.

We had teased Momma so many times about planning everything so much in her notebook that By decided to be cute, and asked, "Uh, could someone check that 'Watsons Go to Birmingham' book and see who's supposed to be holding Joey's leaking head for the first hundred miles in Ohio?"

Momma and Dad looked at each other and laughed, and I did too. I really don't know why bullies have such a good sense of humor.

It didn't matter who won the argument 'cause the car started rocking me to sleep. Maybe someone could say the Brown Bomber was old and ugly, but you could never say anything bad about its seats, they were the best things in the world. I leaned my head back and watched Ohio go zipping by.

I couldn't keep my head from sinking deeper and deeper into the Brown Bomber's seat.

I woke up and got real nervous real fast. I felt something wet in my pants starting to run down my leg. I opened my eyes and said, "Whew!" It was just Joey drooling all over me. I complained and Momma made By take Joey's head for a while.

I took her shoes off for her, and inside one of her shoes was a kind of worn-down picture of a little white boy with a girl's hairdo and a smiling dog. In a circle around both of them it said, "Buster Brown."

As I drifted back to sleep I wondered what a little white boy would think if he knew he was getting stepped on every day by my sister. Then my neck got rubberized again and my head nodded down.

It nodded back up when I heard Momma say real soft to Dad, "How you doing? Cincinnati's just ahead."

"Oh, I'm fine. I've still got a lot in me. I think I'll just stop in Cincy for a stretch and some gas."

"Really?" Momma didn't sound too happy.

"Sure, why not? The kids are all asleep and you looked like you were about gone yourself."

Momma didn't say anything, but I knew she'd have to change her plans if we didn't stop for the night in Cincinnati. Dad kept trying to make it seem O.K. He smiled and said, "Don't worry, Wilona, we might as well go just a little further."

I wanted to lean up and whisper to Momma that I knew what Dad was planning, but the last time I was asleep Byron had put Joey's head back in my lap and I was just too lazy to move her. But I knew if I wasn't so sleepy I could tell Momma what I'd heard Dad and Mr. Johnson saying before we left.

Mr. Johnson knew a lot about cars so Dad asked him to take a good look at the Bomber before we went to Alabama. I was sitting in the car pretending I was driving and Dad and Mr. Johnson were under the hood.

"Oh, yeah, Daniel, this baby's sound as a dollar."

"Well, let me ask you something, Theo," Dad had said. "Do you think she could run it to Alabama straight?"

"Hmmm." Mr. Johnson thought for a minute. "I don't see why not. As long as you keep your eye on the oil and the water it shouldn't give you a lick of trouble. The question isn't the car, the question is could *you* do it straight?"

"Well, the most I've done before is eight hours and Wilona says this will take about fifteen, but I've talked to some people in the shop and they say it shouldn't be too tough. A couple of them are from Texas and they say they've driven it straight. Alabama's closer, so . . . why not?"

"This Plymouth can do it if you can, Daniel."

"Good. Besides, think of the money we'll save. I'ma give it a shot, but I'm not going to tell Wilona, she'd die. She's got this whole trip planned down to the last minute."

Dad made his voice go kind of high and Southern. "And Daniel, between Lexington and Chattanooga you will inhale 105,564 times and you'll blink 436,475 times—that is, of course, unless you see something exciting, in which case you'll inhale 123,876 times and blink 437,098 times!"

Dad and Mr. Johnson cracked up.

As we were going into Cincinnati I wanted to lean up and whisper to Momma, "Hang on, Momma, you're going to blink and inhale about sixty-two zillion more times before you get out of this car!" But the warm air and the highway noise and the Brown Bomber's seat and the way Joey was breathing all pushed me back to sleep.

I was out through most of Kentucky even though we stopped at some more Ohio-style rest stops. I was so tired that I even used a couple of outhouses, but I kept the door open and made Dad stand outside so in case I fell in he'd be able to pull me out.

The next time I woke up we were pulled over at a Tennessee rest stop. There were no bathrooms and no outhouses or anything, just a pump and a picnic table. When Dad turned the headlights off everything disappeared into the blackest night anyone had ever seen.

As we looked out of the windows Momma checked her notebook, then announced, "This is the Appalachia Mountains. We're over six thousand feet above sea level, this is higher than we've ever been before." And she didn't sound real happy about it either.

All four doors of the Brown Bomber opened and the Weird Watsons got out. As soon as everyone was awake enough to look around we all bunched and hugged up around Momma and Dad, even cool Byron.

Dad laughed. "What's wrong with you guys?"

"Daddy, look how scary it is here!" Joey said, pointing at all the giant shapes in the darkness.

"Nonsense, Punkin, those are just the mountains."

What Dad was calling "just the mountains" were the scariest things I'd ever seen. On every side of us were great big, black hills, and behind these were even bigger, blacker hills, and behind these were the biggest, blackest hills. It looked like someone had crumpled up a pitch-black blanket and dropped the Weird Watsons down into the middle of it.

The air up this high didn't seem right either. It made you feel like something bad was going to happen. If this was a movie there would be loud, scary organ music playing right now.

"Mommy," Joey asked, sounding real scared, "where did all these stars come from?"

We all looked up and instead of seeing the normal amount of stars it looked like there had been a star explosion. There were more stars in the sky than empty space.

"That's because the air is so clean here. This looks like the sky in Birmingham."

Up close to us in the rest stop all we could see was the pump. It looked like a deformed, evil, one-armed space robot. As our eyes got used to the dark we could also see the picnic table and behind it that black woods.

Most of the time Momma and Dad don't like arguing in public but Momma was real hot. She said, "Well, do you see what your nonstop driving has done? Do you see? Instead of being in a motel you've driven us straight into Hell!"

That got everyone's attention because Momma almost never cusses. This really scared me. I know it's stupid, but before I could stop myself I said, "Hell? I thought you said this was Tennessee!"

Joey started boo-hooing right away.

After we nervously nibbled on snacks (everyone sat on the same side of the picnic table), me and By had to go to the bathroom in the woods.

We found two trees where we could keep our eye on each other and I said, "By, do you think there are snakes out here?"

"Snakes? I ain't scared of no snakes, it's the people I'm worried about."

I stopped looking at the ground and began watching the black woods. "What people?" I wished I'd picked a tree closer to Byron.

"Didn't you hear Momma say this was Appalachia?"

"So?"

"Man, they got crackers and rednecks up here that ain't never seen no Negroes before. If they caught your ass out here like this they'd hang you now, then eat you later."

"What's a redneck?"

"A hillbilly. Only worse. Some of 'em don't even speak English."

We made a break for the Brown Bomber. If Byron was trying to scare me he was scaring himself too. I went too fast, though, and I felt a couple of warm drips dribbling down my leg. This time I couldn't blame it on Joey's drooling either. But I didn't care. Having a little pee in your pants had to be better than being dinner for some redneck.

We loaded the car back up and no one really relaxed until Dad drove back out on I-75 and turned the headlights on. The lights knocked some of the darkness out of the way and we felt safe again. Everybody was better and laughing and talking a mile a minute.

"I can't believe how this air feels!" Dad said.

He was right, everything smelled light and green.

"Whose turn is it on the Ultra-Glide?"

"Mine!" I yelled. I handed Momma "Yakety Yak" and they all moaned.

Dad stuck his hand out of the window just as the song came on and said, "Feel that coolness. It feels like you're running your fingers through silk."

Me, Momma, Joey and even Daddy Cool all did what Dad told us to do, and Dad was right, it felt great.

"Wiggle your fingers in it," Dad said.

We all did, and the air seemed slippery and cool as it blew on your hand.

"We're so high and the air is so perfect that do you know what I think we're doing?" Dad asked.

"What?"

"I think we've got our fingers in God's beard and as we drive along we're tickling him."

Byron acted like he was going to throw up.

As we drove down the mountain with our arms sticking out of the windows and our fingers wiggling in the breeze, I thought the Brown Bomber must look like a bug lying on its back with four skinny brown legs kicking and twitching to try to put it back on its feet.

Whatever we were doing it was the best part of the trip so far. What could be better than driving on a mountain while "Yakety Yak" played and cool, light air blew all over you?

11. Bobo Brazil
Meets the Sheik

The next time I woke up it was just starting to get light and somehow I was in the front seat and Momma was in the back. When my eyes got used to where they were I saw Dad holding the steering wheel with one hand and resting his other one on the mirror outside the car. The green lights from the dashboard made his face look puffed up and tired, but he was smiling to himself.

I knew what woke me up this time. The Ultra-Glide was stuck. As we drove, the record was saying, ". . . and don't forget who's tak . . . and don't forget who's tak . . . and don't forget who's tak . . . and don't forget who's tak . . ."

I started to say something to Dad but he looked pretty happy and before I could open my mouth the record hypnotized me back to sleep.

The next time I woke up it was bright day and Joey was in the front seat drooling all over me. The Ultra-Glide was still saying, ". . . and don't forget who's tak . . ."

Dad must have heard me breathe different 'cause he looked down at me and said, "Well, well, well, look who's decided to come back to life!"

"Hi, Dad, are we there yet?"

"Oh no, *et tu, Brute*? You were my last hope. With By and Joey and your mother popping up every few minutes asking 'Are we there yet?' it's been like a stuck record."

"Dad, it *is* a stuck record."

Dad seemed to notice the record player for the first time. "Ahh, that. Well, Kenny, I'm afraid it's more than a stuck record. Something isn't working right."

He lifted the arm off the record and looked in the backseat at Momma, who was asleep.

"But let's keep that between you and me, O.K.?"

"Sure. How long before we stop?"

"We'll be at Grandma Sands's before you know it."

Joey had been listening to us. "Daddy, that's what you said the last time. How much longer? I'm sick of this old car."

"Not too much longer, honey."

"I'll stay up and keep you company, Dad," I said.

"Yeah, me too," Joey added.

I don't know who conked out first. I didn't remember anything about coming into Alabama. I don't think any of us did, especially Dad.

We'd been in the car so long that Dad had started growing a beard. Little tiny hairs were coming out of his face. Most of them were black but nine or ten of them were white.

Dad was looking real, real bad. He was still smiling to himself but now instead of a real smile it looked like he was gripping his teeth together to get ready to bite something. The worst thing, though, was that he had turned the radio on and was listening to country and western music! He was even tapping his hand on the steering wheel like he was really enjoying it.

"Dad, do you know what you're listening to?"

Dad decided to cut up. "Kenneth, I been thinking about having all of our names changed to country names when we get back to Michigan. I'll be Clem, you'll be Homer, By will be Billy-Bob, Joey will be Daisy Mae and your mother will be . . . uh, your mother will be . . . well, I guess your mother's name can just stay Wilona, I don't think we're going to find a more country name than that one, do you?" Me and Dad cracked up.

Momma's head popped up from the backseat and she said in a super-Southern style, "O.K., Clem, Ah hopes when us get to Birmingham you can 'splain tuh these he-uh babies' granny how come you turnt 'em into little zombies from sittin' in this car so long."

Dad laughed, "Now, Wilona, you know it hasn't been that bad. In fact, I'm gonna admit to something that I probably shouldn't."

Momma rubbed her eyes, then put her hand on top of my head. "You gonna do this here admittin' in front of little Homer he-uh?"

Everybody started waking up and stretching and scratching.

Momma kept teasing Dad. "And what 'bout some vittles, Clem, the sun been up fo' hours and you ain't even been out to check them traplines to see if we's gonna have some coon pie fuh bruk-fuss."

Dad yelled out, "Yee-haa!" and then said, "Haven't any of you wondered why you've been sleeping like a little herd of angels?"

Byron said, "Like there was anything to keep anybody awake in this carful of squares."

"Anyway," Dad said, "I'ma let the cat out of the bag. I've been using two kinds of mind power to keep this trip going so smooth. First, after a while I started locking into the road and there was nothing to it! Just me, the road and the Brown Bomber, all tuned in to one hum, and as long as I listened to that hum everything was fine.

"My biggest worry was you, Wilona. I knew after 'while you'd figure out that I wasn't going to stop, and you gotta admit you were good and salty about it at first, right?"

"You know I still am." Momma was upset because all of her notebook planning had been wasted.

"But, Wilona, you got to admit that once you figured out how much money we'd save by not stopping you went along with it."

Momma kind of grunted, not saying yes and not saying no.

Dad cleared his throat and rubbed his hand over the little stubbles that were coming out of his chin. We all knew this was a sign that he was going to start acting the fool. He'd tested Momma to see how mad she really was and decided it was safe to play around.

"Yup," he said, rubbing his chin until it made a scratchy, sawing sound, "eighteen big hours in a row! Nearly a thousand miles! I had a load to deliver and"—he punched the air with his fist—"I delivered it. It's just like this great song I heard a couple of miles back, 'Big Daddy Was a Truck-Drivin' Man!' I'm not gonna lie and say it was easy, uh-uh. There was many a time I wanted to stop, but when those times came I'd just think of my old pal, Joe Espinosa, driving all the way to Texas without stopping and I'd keep my foot in that tank.

"Oh yeah, there were times when your mother was giving me looks like she was gonna kill me the first time I slowed down, but I just kept smiling at her and kept the Brown Bomber chugging on. I'd tell her, 'You're right, sweetheart, we'll just go a little bit farther.' And you kids! You talk about some pathetic, tortured-looking little faces. Eighteen hours in a car can age a kid forty years. Yeah, I swear I've been looking in the rearview mirror and wondering where my babies were and where these three bad-dispositioned, sour-faced, middle-age midgets came from. But your sorry little mugs couldn't stop me either.

"In spite of all the cryin' and bawlin' and moanin' and wailin' and gnashin' of teeth I kept pushing on."

Dad must have been real tired, he hardly ever talked this much straight.

"I got to admit to the other trick I used too, but I can't take full credit for this one."

I hoped Dad was going to say that I helped him by keeping him company, but, "No, some of the credit has to go to *Scientific Popular*." That was the name of a magazine that came to Dad in the mail every month. It had real cool covers, there were always drawings of smiling white people on it standing next to cars with wings or sitting in private submarines or eating a whole meal in one little pill. The covers were real interesting but the insides were real boring.

"Yup, good old *Scientific Popular*, they had an article about sound frequencies and said that certain sounds caused certain effects in all living things, even Weird Watsons! It said the sound of one of those vacuum cleaners can put a baby to sleep. And it works!"

Momma laughed a little. It was strange for all of us to see Dad talking so much.

"When we first hit Alabama and had a bunch of miles to go and you kids were popping up like prairie dogs and crying and saying, 'How much longer?' and 'Mommy, make him stop!' and 'Is that Birmingham over there?' all I did was use that vacuum trick.

"I started buzzin' like a Hoover vacuum and you guys dropped off in reverse seniority! First Joey dropped, then Kenneth, then Daddy Cool, then even you, Wilona!

"Shoot, you guys were out cold from the state line on! I threw a blanket over you in the backseat and then even those whines and whimpers and moans you guys were making didn't bother me.

"And you, Wilona, once I got buzzing, the only thing that was coming out of your mouth was drool!"

"Is that what that sound was?" Momma asked. "I thought you were driving so long you'd lost your mind. I'm still not sure you haven't."

Everybody woke up but it was a fake wake-up, we were all soon back asleep, even though it was morning.

The next thing I remember I was waking up back in the backseat and Momma was saying real, real Southern, "Babies, we home!"

Momma was honking the horn of the Brown Bomber like she was crazy.

I raised my head out of the seat to look at what Momma was calling home and couldn't believe it!

Birmingham looked a lot like Flint! There were real houses, not little log cabins, all over the place! And great big beautiful trees. Most of all, though, there was the sun.

Me, Joetta and Byron unfolded ourselves into the Alabama heat and it was like we all remembered at once that we were going to finally see what Grandma Sands really looked like!

We all bunched up together by Momma's door but she didn't get out, she was still honking the horn like a nut! We had to cover our ears.

Dad said, "Nothing's changed."

The door of a regular little old house opened.

Me and Joey had never seen Grandma Sands in our lives. Byron said he could remember that she was the meanest, ugliest person in the world but he was probably lying, he was only four the last time Momma and Dad were here. Byron said he'd had nightmares for a couple of weeks after they left Alabama ten years ago.

All the Weird Watsons had real good imaginations but none of us was ready for what came out of the door of that house.

I was expecting a troll. I thought Grandma Sands would be bigger than Dad, I thought she'd be foaming at the mouth like she had rabies.

I remember a couple of years ago how Momma had cried and cried when someone called from Alabama and told us that Grandma Sands had had a little stroke, so I knew she walked with a cane now. I'd imagined the cane would be as big as a tree trunk with crows and owls and lizards living in it.

What came out was a teeny-weeny, old, old, old woman that looked just like Momma would if someone shrank her down about five sizes and sucked all the juice out of her!

Grandma Sands waved a little skinny stick in the air and said, "What are you all doin' here today? You ain't supposed to be here till Monday!" Man, if you think Momma can talk Southern-style, you should hear Grandma Sands!

Momma was blubbering and smiling and covering her mouth with both hands and ran right up on the porch and nearly broke that little old woman in half.

"How you doin', Momma?" She cried on the woman's shoulders, then held Grandma Sands out to look at her. "You look so good!"

Boy, Momma can lie when she wants to!

"Y'all come on over here and give your granny a hug," my Southern-style mother said.

Me and Joey and Byron shuffled over in a little crowd and when we got through pushing each other forward I was at the front and had to go on the porch to hug Grandma Sands first.

I tried to be real careful with her. She was just a little taller than me and skinnier than anything I'd ever seen alive. I could see her brown scalp right through her curly silver hair.

Grandma Sands squeezed me hard and cried all over me. She wiped a bunch of tears away with a twisted-up hand and blinked a couple of times before she looked at me. She was so short she didn't even have to look down!

She tried to say something but she couldn't talk, she just stuck her bottom lip out some and nodded her head up and down a couple of times, then pulled me back to her and squeezed me like crazy.

Momma slapped the back of my head and said, "Kenneth Bernard Watson, you'd best quit actin' so silly and give your grandmother a good hug!"

I squeezed her a little. A smell like baby powder came out of her when I did. I really think I could feel her lungs when I touched her back!

I don't know what got Joey started but she was off to

the races with her tears. She was the only one who'd practiced what she'd say to Grandma Sands. She sniffed a couple of times then said, "Hi, Grandma Sands, it's a real pleasure to meet you." You could only half understand what she was saying, she was blubbering so much.

Grandma Sands matched Joey tear for tear. They squeezed each other for a while, then Grandma Sands got her little, squeaky voice back and said to Momma, "Lord, 'Lona, if this child ain't you! Look at this baby, just as pretty and sweet as you!"

Momma and Joey grinned like two nuts.

Byron was next.

This was what I'd dreamed about. These were the two meanest, most evil people I'd ever known and I knew only one of them was going to come out of this alive!

There was going to be a battle something like if Godzilla met King Kong, or if Frankenstein met Dracula, or like when Bobo Brazil meets the Sheik!

I'd imagined that a week or two after we got back to Flint we'd get a phone call from Alabama with the winner of the big battle on the other end.

If it was Byron, he'd talk kind of cool and low out of the corner of his mouth and say, "Shooot, man, you better come get this old chick, I ate her alive."

If Grandma Sands won the battle we'd have to hold the phone away from our ear while she shouted, "'Lona, you call this a bad child? This li'l saint is ready to come back North and go to Sunday school and scrub all y'all's floors!"

But as soon as I saw Grandma Sands I knew that Byron would destroy this poor old woman. I was even afraid Momma might decide not to leave him in Alabama.

Byron walked up on the porch real cool and kind of bent over to give Grandma Sands a hug. Grandma Sands squeezed him hard.

"'Lona, what you teach these babies up North? Don't they know how to give no one a proper hug?" She held Byron by the arms and looked at him from top to bottom. "You grew up to be a fine-lookin' boy. You was so puny when you was born you nearly worried us crazy. Got strong too." She slapped Byron's arm and he kind of laughed.

Grandma Sands reached up and ran her wrinkly old hand over Byron's head. "A little short on hair, but we gonna get on just fine, what you think, By?"

"Yes, ma'am."

"Good, good, see, there's lots of things you can do down here, Mr. Robert ain't as much help as he used to be, so all them things he used to do you can do now."

Momma said, "Who? Mr. who?"

Dad came up on the porch and got a ton of hugs and tears too, then Grandma Sands pulled everybody together. Her little arms could only get around one person at a time but as the Weird Watsons stood there with some of us laughing, some of us crying and some of us

159

looking cool it felt like we all were wrapped up in a big ball.

Grandma Sands kept saying, "My family, my beautiful, beautiful family," except with that Southern-style accent and all the weeping it sounded like she was saying "fambly."

Finally the crowd started breaking up and Grandma Sands said, "Now what am I gonna feed y'all? I wasn't expecting you till Monday. Me and Mr. Robert usually just has leftovers on Sunday, but I guess if By'll go down to Jobe's and pick up some things we can have chicken tonight. You good at following directions, Byron?"

"Huh?" By's face twisted up.

"What?" Grandma Sands's voice popped like one of those big brown grocery bags being snapped open.

By looked surprised and said, "I meant, 'Huh, *ma'am'*"

"You good at following directions? Jobe's is a good little walk."

I said, "He can follow directions real good, Grandma Sands, he's not as dumb as he looks."

I shut up real quick and wished I hadn't said anything when Grandma Sands looked at me and said, "'Lona, maybe there's two who should be spending the summer down here with their granny."

Everybody started going inside the ugly little house. Momma sounded worried. "Momma, who is this Mr. Robert?"

Grandma Sands laughed just like the Wicked Witch of the West and said, "Honey, we got to talk. You jus' be patient and soon's he gets up I want all of y'all to meet him."

"Soon's he gets up? Awww, Momma . . ." Momma sounded real upset and disappointed and Southern.

But not as disappointed as me.

The way Byron kept his head down and was smiling and saying "Yes, ma'am" this and "No, ma'am" that, it looked like he had surrendered before the first punch was thrown.

Instead of King Kong and Godzilla it was like King Kong and Bambi; instead of Bobo Brazil and the Sheik it was like Bobo Brazil and Captain Kangaroo; instead of Dracula and Frankenstein it was like Dracula and a giraffe, and Byron was all neck.

He knew exactly what I was thinking.

After Grandma Sands gave us directions Byron looked at me sideways and said, "What you starin' at, square?"

I just shook my head.

"What you expect?" By asked. "You seen her. That bird's as old as dirt. She's so old I bet she used to step over dinosaur turds. I ain't gonna have her death on my hands."

I knew that was a lie.

It seemed like all of the fight was out of Byron and we'd only been in Birmingham for a couple of minutes.

12. That Dog
Won't Hunt No More

Birmingham was like an oven. That first night I couldn't sleep at all, me and By had to share a bed and we both were sweating like two pigs. It got so hot that Byron didn't even keep a sheet on himself to make sure I didn't accidentally touch him in the night. He finally slept on the floor because he said it was a little bit cooler.

When I got up Byron was gone. I looked out of the window into the backyard and By and Dad and Mr. Robert were standing under a great big tree with a dog. I went to the bathroom real quick, did my morning scratches, then ran out to be with the guys.

"Morning, Kenny."

"Morning, Dad. Morning, Mr. Robert. Morning, By."

Byron just grunted, then said, "Man, you gotta quit drinking so much water, you sweated up the whole bed last night, I ain't sharing the bed with your leaky little bu—"—he looked at Dad—"with your leaky little self again."

Mr. Robert said, "You boys'll get used to the heat."

Dad petted the dog and said, "He's too old to hunt?"

"Oh yeah, that dog won't hunt no more. He's just like me, lost the desire. Both of us got to the point where we just couldn't pull the trigger. Both of us got to be just like Joe Louis toward the end. Remember his last fights, Daniel? Remember how Joe'd just walk around the ring waving that left fist like a threat, he just couldn't throw it, he just couldn't pull the trigger no more, his mind told him to do it but his body wouldn't cooperate. That's me and Toddy. There's times at night I hear him howl and I know he's dreaming about being back in the woods, but both of us know that's gone."

Mr. Robert bent down and rubbed the dog's head. "Yeah, son, in his day this was the best coon dog in all Alabama. Used to get a hundred bucks just to stud him."

Byron rubbed the old, gray, nasty-looking dog's head too. "A hundred bucks? Man!"

"Yeah, me and Toddy saved each other's lives, hate seeing him get so old." Judging by the way Mr. Robert looked I bet the dog was saying the same thing about him.

"How'd you save his life?"

"You ever been coon hunting?"

"No, sir."

"Well, there ain't too many animals wilier or tougher

than a old coon. Most people think you just chase 'em up a tree and pop 'em, but that ain't half the story.

"Toddy'd trailed this coon all the way out to this lake, and the coon went in the water. Now most of the time a dog'll stop right at the water, they know better than to go in, but Toddy must've just dove right in after that coon. He musta been a half mile ahead of me when I heard him holler and then get real quiet."

"What happened?"

"The coon got him in the water and held his head under till he drownded him."

I stopped believing this junk right there. A raccoon drowning a dog? I looked at By and Dad but they both were believing what Mr. Robert was saying.

Dad said, "I've heard about raccoons doing that."

"Oh yeah, Toddy here's living proof."

Byron said, "If he drowned how come he ain't dead?"

"Well, when I finally got to that lake I seen the coon going out one way and Toddy nowhere in sight, and I knew what happened. I dove right in that water and started looking for him. Took me only a minute. I dragged him back to shore, turnt him upside down to let the water run outta him, held his mouth shut and breathed right in his nose. He kicked a couple of times, then came to."

Byron said, "Man! That's too much! That's cool!"

All I could think of was that Mr. Robert was probably the only human being who'd ever put his mouth on a dog's nose. That was pretty cool!

I asked Dad, "When do we eat?"

"Kenny, you're the only one who hasn't eaten already. Your mother and grandmother are in the kitchen, go on in."

I went back inside.

Even before I got in I could hear Momma saying that Birmingham wasn't anything like what she remembered. Her favorite sayings got to be "What's this?" and "How long's this been like that?" and "When did that happen?" and "Why do you do this like that?" and, most of all, "Awww, Momma . . ."

Grandma Sands thought Momma was hilarious and cracked up every time Momma got upset or worried about something that she didn't remember or didn't like. Grandma Sands must have seen *The Wizard of Oz* a million times because every time she laughed it sounded just like that Wicked Witch of the West. At first her laugh was so scary that whenever me and Joey heard it we wanted to go get behind something or someone. But after a while we got used to it.

It took us even longer to get used to the Southern style of talking. Man! Grandma Sands and Momma would get yakking to each other and we could only understand half of the things that they said.

The smell of bacon dragged me right into the kitchen. Momma, Joey and Grandma Sands were sitting at the little, skinny kitchen table yakking.

"Morning, Kenneth."

"Morning, Momma. Morning, Joey. Morning, Grandma Sands."

"You sleep O.K.?"

"It was real hot."

Joey was sitting in Momma's lap looking all drowsy. She said, "I know, I was sweating all night."

The bacon was sitting on a plate on a piece of paper towel. Momma had another piece of paper towel in her hands because all the things that Grandma Sands was telling her were making her hands get all sweaty and disgusting. I got some cereal and bread and bacon and sat at the skinny table with them.

I must have interrupted something real important because as soon as I sat down Momma acted like I'd disappeared and started asking Grandma Sands more questions. "Well, what about Calla Lily Lincoln? I always wondered what she's doing. . . ."

"'Lona, didn't I write to you about that? Uh, uh, uh . . ."

They kept on talking and kept on ooohing and aahing and Grandma Sands kept on interrupting breakfast by scaring me and Joey with that laugh and Momma kept on saying "Awww, Momma . . ." and she kept on having to get up and get more paper towels to wipe her hands and most of all she kept on talking more and more Southern-style.

They talked about how much trouble people were having with some white people down here, who got married to who, how many kids this one had, how many times that one was in jail, a bunch of boring junk like that. It didn't get interesting until I noticed that Momma got real, real nervous right before she said,

"And what about you, Momma? Mr. Robert seems like a nice man and all, but . . ."

Grandma gave that laugh and my spoon flew out of my hand and spilled corn flakes on the table. Momma acted like she didn't even notice, but without even looking at me she handed me one of the nasty, soaking-wet pieces of paper towel and kept looking at Grandma Sands.

"I was wondering when we'd get to that." Grandma Sands smiled. "We been good friends since right after you-all left for Flint—"

Momma was being kind of rude, she interrupted and said, "Awww, Momma, good friends? What does that mean?"

"Wilona Sands, what is it that's bothering you? Why don't you just say what's on your mind?"

Momma started wringing the neck of another piece of paper towel. "I just don't understand what's going on here. How come I never knew him? Did Daddy know him?" Momma said that last part like she was dropping a bomb on Grandma Sands.

Grandma Sands looked at her for a minute. "'Lona, things are different from what they were when you left. Nearly everything changes. Your daddy's been gone for almost twenty years." Grandma Sands had stopped smiling. "Now Mr. Robert is my dearest friend."

Wow! I could see where Byron learned how to say a couple of words and have people think he'd said a whole bunch more! Grandma Sands didn't yell or scream or anything, but the way she said those couple of things made everybody who heard it shut their mouths and listen real hard. Even though she only told Momma that Mr. Robert was her friend it seemed like I heard her also give my mother a real good scolding. Momma pouted and kissed the top of Joey's head.

I picked up my spoon and kept eating. This was great! I'd never seen Momma act like a little kid who just got yelled at but there she was, picking at a piece of paper towel and looking kind of embarrassed. Dad and Byron came in with Mr. Robert.

"Mr. Robert's going to walk us over to the lake, show us the best fishing spots for later. Joey, Kenny, you coming? Give these two some time alone to talk."

Momma pushed Joey off her lap and we followed the little parade outside.

The heat made me and Joey feel like we couldn't wake up. I didn't want to do any walking but the dirty dogs made me go anyway. The only kid that acted like he was having any fun was Byron. He walked the whole way with Mr. Robert and Dad and laughed and joked with them about every stupid story they told.

When we finally got back I went to sleep under a fan. They were going to force me to go fishing with Byron and Joey the next day and I knew I needed a ton of rest. I started to think that making Byron spend all of his summer in this heat was more punishment than even a juvenile delinquent like him deserved. But he seemed like he was having a great time.

13. I Meet Winnie's Evil Twin Brother, the Wool Pooh

"If y'all are going to the water you stay away from Collier's Landing. A couple of years ago Miss Thomas's little boy Jimmy got caught up in some kinda whirlpool there and they didn't find the poor soul's body for three days."

I'd only halfway listened to what Grandma Sands had said, and now me and Joey and Byron were standing at a sign with arrows that pointed in two directions. The one pointing to the left said "Public Swimming" and the other one, pointing to the right, looked like it had been on the post for a million years but if you got close to it you could read, "WARNING! NO TRESPASSING! NO SWIMING! NO PUBLIC ENTREE! Signed Joe Collier."

"Oh, man! Collier's Landing," I said. "Let's go!" I knew Joey wouldn't like this, but I figured me and By could talk her into coming and not snitching.

Joey said, "Uh-uh, Kenny, you heard Grandma Sands tell about that little boy getting lost in the water. What was that thing called that she said got him?"

Daddy Cool said, "Didn't you hear what she said, Joey? She said he got caught by the Wool Pooh."

"Is that a fish?" Joey asked.

"Uh-uh. You know who Winnie-the-Pooh is, don't you?"

Me and Joey both nodded.

"Well, the Wool Pooh is Winnie's evil twin brother. Don't no one ever write about him 'cause they don't want to scare y'all kids. What he does is hide underwater and snatch stupid kids down with him."

By figured that dumb story was enough to scare me off and he started walking in the direction of the public swimming. "If Kenny wants to take his stupid little behind down there and get snatched, let him." By grabbed Joey's hand and started pulling her along with him, but she skidded her feet in the dirt.

"But Byron, what if the Wool Pooh comes down to where we're going? Can't he swim down there and get people too?"

"Naw, Joey, the Wool Pooh don't come on public beaches, he just grabs folks that are too stingy to let peons come on their land, like this Collier guy."

Who could understand Byron? Here was a chance for another Fantastic Adventure and he was going in the wrong direction. Something was wrong with him. If he was in Flint and you told him not to do something he'd go right out and do it, but now he was acting real dull and square. Maybe it was the heat, maybe just like it had sucked all the energy out of me it had sucked all the meanness and fun out of Byron.

"What you gonna do, punk?" Byron shouted over his shoulder. Joey yelled, "Come on, Kenny! You know what Grandma Sands said."

I couldn't believe it. I really wanted to go see where some kid drowned and now By was choosing this time to listen to what a grown-up told him.

"Awww, man, I'm going to Collier's Landing."

Byron shrugged. "Have fun."

I shouted, "What's wrong with you? When are you going to start acting like you normally do? What would Buphead say if he saw you acting like this?"

Byron flipped me double middle fingers and another finger sign I'd never seen before and said, "Just keep your stupid little butt out of the water."

"Forget you, I'm going!"

They kept walking.

"I'm not playing!"

Joey waved.

"I'm going to Collier's Landing!"

They were gone.

I looked in the direction that the warning sign was pointing and started to get a little nervous. I turned and started to follow Joey and Byron, but finally decided I really was going to go to Collier's Landing. Maybe Byron was getting sick of having more Fantastic Adventures, but I figured I was getting old enough to have some myself.

"You're a couple of jive squares!" I shouted, then walked off the way the warning sign pointed.

Byron must have thought I was stupid. Whoever

171

heard of something called a Wool Pooh? I wasn't sure what the lie was, but I knew Byron had made that junk up. Besides, if Winnie-the-Pooh had an evil twin brother it seemed like I would have read about it somewhere. Some of the time it was kind of hard to understand what Grandma Sands was saying, but I couldn't remember her saying anything about any Wool Pooh. If there really was something that snatched kids into the water Momma and Dad wouldn't have let us come down here, would they?

I knew all that stuff but I was still kind of nervous when I followed the little trail that went through a bunch of bushes and led to the water. I forgot all about Byron's lies as soon as I saw the water. Collier's Landing was great! The water was dark, dark blue, and best of all, it was about a hundred degrees cooler.

Joe Collier had put up another sign on a giant tree: "WARNING! DANGER! NO SWIMING! SIX LIFES BEEN LOST HERE! BAD DROP OFF! Signed Joe Collier."

Six? Grandma Sands had said one little boy drowned here, not six! I felt dumb but I looked real hard at the water to see if the Wool Pooh was hiding there. I even looked up and down the shore to see if there were any strange footprints on the ground. I was kind of worried because this sign looked a lot fresher than the first one.

I kept waiting for By to jump out of the bushes and say something like, "Aha, you little dope, I got you! I made you look for a Wool Pooh!" but everything was real calm and quiet, the water didn't even look like it was moving, but like it was breathing, going up and down, up and down, and it made a sound like the wind blowing through big trees in Flint.

I walked right to the edge of the water and still didn't see anything strange so I figured if there was some real kind of danger Byron would have followed me here and stopped me from getting hurt, wouldn't he?

Then a bell went off in my head. I knew Joe Collier put that sign up because he didn't want to share his lake with anyone! The Wool Pooh was some made-up garbage!

There's one good thing about getting in trouble: It seems like you do it in steps. It seems like you don't just end up in trouble but that you kind of ease yourself into it. It also seems like the worse the trouble is that you get into, the more steps it takes to get there. Sort of like you're getting a bunch of little warnings on the way; sort of like if you really wanted to you could turn around.

The first warning I should have listened to was when Daddy Cool and Joey followed the arrow to the left and I went to the right. The second warning came when I decided to wade in the water and the knots wouldn't come out of my tennis shoe laces and I had to pull and tug the shoes off with the laces still tied. After that it's kind of hard to count how many warnings I got, because with the trouble I ended up in I must've had a zillion of them.

Step by step I kept easing into trouble until I finally

was standing in the lake with the water up to my knees. I'd gone out into the water because there were a bunch of little, stupid-looking, slow-moving fish right near the shore and I thought I might be able to catch some of them and make them pets. I wasn't afraid because I figured if there was a real Wool Pooh and he was in the area these little fish wouldn't be hanging around.

Alabama fish were a lot friendlier, and a lot trickier, than Michigan ones. I bent over and stuck my hand in the water and tried to grab a couple but they kept slipping away like they were covered with soap. They were right there and I couldn't grab them. They didn't even act like they were afraid of me, they just kept swimming around my legs, even bumping their faces into me, like they were trying to kiss me. It seemed like they wanted me to catch them and take them back to Flint.

After missing about a hundred times I stood up and saw the reason the fish wouldn't go out in deeper water. There was a big green turtle, about the size of a football, cruising back and forth in the deep water, and he looked just as slow and stupid as the fish did.

Wow! Who'd want to have a fish for a pet when you could have a turtle?

I took a few more steps out and the cool, blue water came all the way up to my arms. Getting cool all of a sudden like this made me bug my eyes and suck in my breath. I made a quick grab at the stupid turtle and, zoom, he flapped his arms once and disappeared into deeper water.

That quick grab was my last step. Boom, all of a sudden I was in big, big trouble!

The rocky ground under my feet started sliding away from the shore. I didn't get nervous because I knew I could flap my arms like the turtle and get back to the dirt. I looked up and saw the shore was still real close. I flapped my arms and nothing happened, I stayed in the same spot. Then the rocks under my feet were gone and I was kicking in water. With the tips of my toes I could still brush some of the rocks but they were all slipping and sliding away from shore.

I pushed away to try to swim back and my head bobbed under the water. All the sound and light from Alabama disappeared because my eyes automatically shut and it seemed like my ears were stuffed with cotton. I got a mouthful of water but my head came right back up. I laughed because I was spitting and patoohing a mile a minute when my head popped out of the water. But the laughing stopped real quick when I tried swimming again and my head went back under.

That's when I got really scared. I'd seen enough cartoons to know that when your head goes down three times it doesn't ever come up again! I knew if I went down one more time I was as dead as a donut!

My eyes looked at the shore, where my shoes were sitting safe on some rocks. "Awww, man," I said to myself, "I wish I had a magic lamp so I could have the genie make me be where those shoes are and they could be where I am!"

That was the last thing I thought about before I found out that Grandma Sands and Byron and Joe Collier weren't lying at all. That was the last thing I thought about before I found out that the Wool Pooh was real and big and mean and horrible and that he didn't care at all about dragging kids out into the water!

I'd never, ever been this scared in my life! I hollered out, "Momma!" My arms were punching the water like it was a person and my legs were going a mile a minute to try to get back to the shore. But now even my toes couldn't find anything to touch.

"O.K., Kenny," I said to myself, "you know you're going to be all right. Just get real calm and swim back to the land. When you count to three just go back to your shoes." I stopped kicking for a second and said, "One, two, three . . ." Then I gave my arms one more flap to go back to shore and down I went again! My head went under for the third time and I knew I'd never come back up again. Going down three times like this is just like waking up and finding yourself tied to a tree with someone saying, "Ready, aim, fire!"

That's when he came swimming real slow out of the deep, and even though my head was underneath the dark water I could see him coming right at me. He didn't look like he was related to Winnie-the-Pooh at all, he was big and gray with hard square-looking fingers. Where he should have had a face there was nothing but dark gray. Where he should have had eyes there was nothing but a darker colder-looking color. He grabbed my leg and started pulling me down.

I kicked and scratched at him but he was just too strong, it seemed like he didn't even feel my punches! My head felt like it was going to explode; I didn't think I could hold my breath for another second. I was feeling real, real scared and dizzy from holding my breath this long. Then suddenly I could see that there was someone else in the water and the Wool Pooh was pulling me right toward them.

It was a little girl and she had on a real pretty blue dress and big, yellow wings and something tied around her head. When the Wool Pooh pulled me closer I could see that it was a little angel, and wait a minute, it was Joetta, looking just like the angel Mrs. Davidson had given her! Joey had wings and a halo! Her face was real calm too, but she was pointing straight up like there was something important I should look at.

This angel that looked like Joey was telling me I had to swim up one more time.

This really scared me. I knew it wasn't a good sign when you started seeing angels so I kicked and flapped my arms and started going toward the sky! My head came up and I spit out a bellyful of water and took a couple of good, deep breaths.

"Momma! Momma! Help me . . ."

But the Wool Pooh wasn't through with me. I felt his hard, hard hand go around my ankle and I went down for the fourth time!

I got pulled a little further and saw someone else in the water with me, kicking up a ton of dirt and scratching at the water like they were crazy. Byron!

Man! The Wool Pooh is going to let me see all my family one more time before I go!

Byron tried grabbing at me but the Wool Pooh was pulling me away too fast. I saw By's legs swim back up toward the sky.

Pull-*whisshh*-stop, *pull-whisshh*-stop. Up ahead someone else was in the water. It has to be Momma and Dad! Good-bye, Momma! Good-bye, Dad! No, it's By again, still looking all crazy, still scratching the water.

Byron and the Wool Pooh started duking it out. By must have hit it a hundred times in that place where its face should've been. Finally the Wool Pooh couldn't take any more and I felt those hard cold fingers come off my ankle. The Wool Pooh swam back into the deep water. The last thing I noticed about him was that he had big square toes.

Byron grabbed me and put his arm around my neck and it felt like he was trying to choke me.

As soon as he got me on the shore and turned me upside down I felt like I was going to die! I started throwing up a ton of water and food. If there was a forest fire somewhere all they would have to do is hold me over it and I would have put it out! I threw up and coughed and choked and vomited about a million times, and all this just because I'd breathed in some air!

By held my ankles and kept banging me up and down and screaming at me. When the sound from the water in my ears and the sound of me vomiting my guts out and the *whisshh* sound from the Wool Pooh finally left me I could hear Byron shouting, ". . . Awww, man, awww, man, awww, man . . ." over and over.

Finally I yelled, "Stop! Put me down!"

Byron dropped me on the ground right on top of all the water and junk that I'd thrown up. I knew he was going to make a stupid joke about me landing face-first in all that mess but he didn't, he just wrapped his arms around my shoulders real tight and put his mouth right on top of my head! Byron was shaking like he was getting electrocuted and crying like a baby and kissing the top of my head over and over!

This was real disgusting. He just kept saying, "Kenny, Kenny, Kenny . . . ," a bunch of times with his mouth wide open on top of my head. I could feel his teeth grinding into my skull but By didn't care.

I said, "Awww, man . . ." and tried to make him quit but all I could do was sit there too tired to do anything but let Daddy Cool nibble on the top of my head while he cried like a kindergarten baby.

14. Every Bird and Bug in Birmingham Stops and Wonders

I know it was Sunday because I heard Joetta getting ready for Sunday school. The neighbors came and got her as soon as I got out of bed. I was standing in the doorway of the bedroom doing my morning scratches when she walked by.

"Hi, Kenny. See you later."

"Bye, Joey."

She had on a fluffy white skirt, a regular blouse and the little white gloves Grandma Sands had made her. I don't know why, but I said, "Joey . . ."

She stopped. "Huh?"

I couldn't think why I called her name so I just kind of threw out, "You look real pretty."

She smiled and thanked me. She did look kind of pretty too, she had on a lacy white hat and little lacy white socks and her shiny, shiny black shoes.

The people that came to get her saw me and one of them said, "How come you ain't coming to Sunday school, young man?"

I smiled and said, "I forgot to get up in time."

Everybody in the house knew that was a lie but no one seemed to care. I wondered if there was something wrong with me, because it was real easy for me to lie, even to a pack of religious people on Sunday morning.

I had my cereal and went out into the backyard. It was too hot even this early in the morning, so I walked over to the giant magnolia tree and rested in the coolness of its shade.

All of the energy was gone from me already. It had been a few days since I almost got snatched by the Wool Pooh and I still felt weak and tired all the time.

Byron had made me promise not to tell anyone what had happened so everybody thought I was just being lazy. I heard people waking up and moving around inside but I was feeling too tired to go and speak to anyone.

Momma stuck her head out of the back door and got ready to yell for me but when she saw me plopped down at the foot of the tree she smiled. "Well, Kenneth, I thought you'd wandered off. How are you this morning?"

"It was too hot to sleep."

"Think you can last one more week?"

"Uh-uh."

"Well, isn't this better than winter up North?"

"Quit teasing, Momma, you know it isn't. I wish I was back in our igloo in Flint."

She laughed and the screen door closed behind her.

I started going to sleep under the tree and thought I was dreaming when the noise came.

I felt it more than heard it. The giant old magnolia tree shook one time like something had given it a hard snatch by the roots. Then there was a sound like a far-off thunderstorm coming. Except it only thundered one long time.

It seemed like every animal and bird and bug in Birmingham stopped making noise for about two seconds. It seemed like everything that was alive stopped whatever it was doing and was wondering the same thing: What was that noise?

Doors opened in the neighborhood and people came out and looked up in the sky but there was nothing there, not one cloud, nothing to give a clue to what the big hollow sound was, nothing but bright, hot, stupid Alabama sun.

Dad came to the back door, in pajama pants and a T-shirt. "What was that? Was that back here?"

I shook my head. He looked like a bell went off in his head and said, "Oh Lord, where's Byron?"

Byron poked his head out of the door, still in his underpants and still doing his morning scratches. "What?" he said. "I didn't do nothing. I was asleep. What was that bang?"

Dad kept looking toward the sky and said, "Hmm, must have been a sonic boom."

He closed the screen door.

If this had happened in Flint I would have investigated to find out what it was, but that horrible sun had sucked all the curiosity out of me.

I leaned back against the tree and closed my eyes. I don't know if I got to sleep or not but Momma's scream made me jump nearly to the magnolia's top branch. I'd never heard Momma's voice sound so bad. I felt like I did that time I stuck a bobby pin in a wall socket.

I ran to the door and into the house and By almost knocked me over running back toward the bedroom.

"What's wrong with Momma?" I asked.

I looked in the living room but Momma and Dad weren't there. I ran back to the bedroom, where Byron was trying to wrestle into a pair of pants.

"By! What happened?"

He got the pants up and said, "A guy just came by and said somebody dropped a bomb on Joey's church." And he was gone, exploding out of the front door trying to zip up his pants at the same time he ran off the porch.

Some of the time I wondered if something really was wrong with me. Byron had just told me that someone had dropped a bomb on Joey's church, hadn't he? If that was true why did I just stand there looking stupid? If that was true why was I only thinking about how much trouble By was going to be in when they heard how loud he'd slammed the screen door, and asking myself why hadn't he put on his shoes? His socks wouldn't last two minutes on the Alabama mud.

I ran out onto the porch and into the street. It looked

like someone had set off a people magnet, it seemed like everyone in Birmingham was running down the street, it looked like a river of scared brown bodies was being jerked in the same direction that By had gone, so I followed.

I guess my ears couldn't take it so they just stopped listening. I could see people everywhere making their mouths go like they were screaming and pointing and yelling but I didn't hear anything. I saw Momma and Dad and Byron holding on to each other, all three of them looking like they were crazy and trying to keep each other away from the pile of rocks that used to be the front of the church. Momma was so upset that she even forgot to cover the space in her front teeth. I couldn't hear her but I'd bet a million dollars she was shouting, "Why?" over and over like a real nut. It looked like Dad's mouth was yelling, "Joetta!"

I was kind of surprised no adult stopped me from walking right up to the church.

I got right next to where the door used to be when the guy came out with a little girl in his arms. He had on the same thing Dad did, a T-shirt and pajama pants, but it looked like he'd been painting with red, red paint. The little girl had on a blue dress and little blue frilly socks and black shiny, shiny shoes.

I looked into the church and saw smoke and dust flying around like a tornado was in there. One light from the ceiling was still hanging down by a wire, flickering and swinging back and forth, and every once in a while I could see stuff inside. I could see a couple of grown-ups moving around looking lost, trying to pick things up, then the smoke would cover them, and then the bulb would flicker out and they'd disappear. I could see Bibles and coloring books thrown all over the place, then they'd get covered by the smoke. I could see a shiny, shiny black shoe lying halfway underneath some concrete, then it got covered with smoke, and then the lightbulb flickered out again.

I bent down to pull the shoe from under the concrete and tugged and pulled at it but it felt like something was pulling it back.

All the hair on my head jumped up to attention. The light flickered back on and the smoke cleared and I could see that hanging on to the other end of the shoe was a giant gray hand with cold, hard square fingers.

Oh-oh. I looked up and saw a familiar guy and before he got covered with smoke he looked at me and I saw he had big square shoulders and nothing where his face should have been. The Wool Pooh.

Oh, man. I gave the shoe one more hard tug and it popped loose from a frilly white sock. I got real scared. I walked as slow and as quiet as I could out of the church. Maybe if I moved quiet enough he wouldn't come for me. Maybe if I walked and didn't look back he'd leave me alone. I walked past where the adults were still screaming and pointing, I walked past where that guy had set the little girl in blue, right next to where some-one else had set a little girl in red. I knew if Joey sat down next to those two their dresses would make the red, white and blue of the American flag. Grown-ups were kneeling down by them and the adults' hands fluttered down toward the little girls, then, before they touched anything, fluttered back up, over and over. Their hands looked like a little flock of brown sparrows that were too nervous to land.

I walked past people lying around in little balls on the grass crying and twitching, I walked past people squeezing each other and shaking, I walked past people hugging trees and telephone poles, looking like they were afraid they might fly off the earth if they let go. I walked past a million people with their mouths wide-opened and no sounds coming out. I didn't look behind me and walked back as quick as I could to Grandma Sands's house.

I felt like I floated up the front stairs, then I made sure the screen door didn't slam and took my shoes off and went in and sat on my bed. I hadn't remembered to make it that morning so I got up and tucked the sheets in and fluffed up the pillow like Momma does. I sat back on the bed and looked down at my hands. They were acting like nervous little sparrows too so I squeezed them between my knees.

I reached in my pocket and took out the shiny, shiny shoe. When me and the Wool Pooh were trying to grab it away from each other the back part had gotten ripped. Man! The shoe was ripped like it was made out of paper! The picture of the little white boy with the girl's hairdo and the dog was torn right in half. All that was left was the dog, smiling at me like he'd just eaten a cat.

I tried to remember if I'd been mean to Joey this morning. I guessed I hadn't. I never did tell her how she helped Byron save my life in the water. I guessed I should have.

"Where'd you go? How'd you get back here so fast? How come you changed your clothes?" My ears had decided to work again.

I looked up toward the door but stopped looking when I saw the white, white frilly socks standing on the wooden floor in front of my door. I guessed the Wool Pooh was taking Joey around for her last visits. I was afraid to look up, I was afraid to look at her face, I knew I'd see the Wool Pooh's rope tied around her waist.

"Hi, Joey" was all I could think of saying.

"Where're Momma and Daddy?"

"Oh. You'll probably get to see them next. He takes you around to see your family before you go."

She sat beside me on the bed. I still wouldn't look at her. I dropped the shoe and used my knees to stop the sparrows from fluttering around.

Oh, man! This was very scary. I'd seen the two little girls on the grass in the red and blue dresses and I didn't want to see my little sister that way too.

"What's wrong with you, Kenny? How come you're looking so funny?"

"I guess I should have told you thanks for saving my life, huh? Is it too late to tell you that?"

Joey didn't say anything for a second, then got up off the bed. "Why're you acting so crazy? Where're Mommy and Daddy? What's that you dropped? What're you trying to hide?"

She picked her shoe up from where I'd dropped it.

"Oooh, Kenny, whose shoe is this? What did you do to it?"

"It's yours, Joey, I got it from the Wool Pooh."

"You better quit trying to scare me, Kenny, or I'm gonna tell Momma! This better not be my shoe or you're in big trouble, buster."

Joey walked out of the room but I still couldn't look at her. The Wool Pooh was *pull-whisshh*-stopping her away.

"Joey!"

After a second she came back into my bedroom. "What?" She was sounding real, real mean.

I didn't look up. I kept looking at my hands. "I love you."

Whop! The shiny, shiny, ripped black shoe hit me right in my chest. "Whose shoe is that?"

I finally looked up to see what Joey looked like. There were no ropes around her waist and nobody with square toes was hanging around. But what really surprised me was that Joey had both of her shiny, shiny black shoes in her hands. She'd taken them off at the front door.

"Kenneth Bernard Watson, you better tell me what's going on or I'm really gonna tell! I'm not playing with you!" Joey was imitating Momma so much that she didn't say "Bernard," she said "Buh-Nod."

"Joey, didn't you go to Sunday school?"

"You know I did."

"Don't you know what happened?"

Joey sat back down next to me. "Kenny, I'm not playing with you, why are you acting so weird?" Her voice was starting to get all choky.

"Why aren't you still in that church?"

"It was so hot in there that I went and stood on the porch and saw you."

"Saw me? Where?"

"Kenny, you'd better stop this nonsense. You know you waved at me from across the street, you know when I tried to come to you you kept laughing and running in front of me, you know I chased you all the way down that street!" Joey got a funny look on her face. "But you had on different clothes." Joey's voice was getting higher with everything she said, and when she was done she was sounding real crazy.

"Joey, I—"

"That's it! You're through this time, mister. You don't know when to stop teasing, do you? That's it, I'm telling on you!"

Joey stood up and ran up the stairs screaming, "Mommy! Mommy! Mommy!"

I could hear Grandma Sands moving around upstairs and she finally clomped down the steps and came into my room. Joey was hanging on her arm still screaming.

Grandma Sands must have real thin blood, because even though it was hot as a furnace in the house she had on a big thick nightgown and a big thick robe. The smell of baby powder came into the room a second after she did.

"What on earth are y'all doing raising this much Cain this early in the morning? Joetta honey, stop that noise. Kenny, what's wrong with this child?"

Joetta finally said, "He's trying to scare me, Grandma Sands, he won't tell me where Mommy is!" Joey kept boo-hooing like a real idiot.

"Kenneth, where's Wilona and Daniel?" Grandma Sands pulled Joey off her leg and held her shoulders, then gave her a little shake. "Joetta, you stop that noise! Grandma Sands can't handle that much noise this early, sweetheart."

A bell went off in my head! The Wool Pooh had missed Joey! He wasn't having much luck at all with any of the Weird Watsons! I had to go to the church to get Momma and Dad and Byron!

Grandma Sands said, "What are all them sirens doing? Lord, has the whole world gone mad today? Where's your momma and daddy?"

The last thing I heard was Grandma Sands yelling, "Boy, if you slam that door like that again . . ." I looked down and saw my socks flying over the Alabama mud.

15. The World-Famous Watson Pet Hospital

Momma and Dad didn't know I was in the living room. We'd been back in Flint for a couple of weeks and they were still talking about what had happened, but never around us. The only thing I knew for sure was that the bomb wasn't dropped on the church by an airplane. Grandma Sands called a couple of times and told them that the police thought two white men drove by in a car and threw it in during services, or that they'd already hidden it in the church with a clock set to go off during Sunday school. However it got in the church it had killed four little girls, blinded a couple more and sent a bunch of other people to the hospital. I couldn't stop wondering if those two little girls I saw on the lawn were okay.

From my secret hiding place in the living room I could listen to Momma and Dad and it seemed like they spent most of the time trying to figure out how they could explain to us what happened. Some of the time they were mad, some of the time they were calm and some of the time they just sat on the couch and cried.

Even though none of us kids got hurt by the bomb they acted like they were worried about us. They weren't too worried about Byron and weren't worried at all about Joey, we'd all agreed not to tell her what happened at that church and had left Birmingham that night, before she had a chance to find anything out. I was kind of surprised because the way Momma and Dad were talking I could tell they were most worried about me.

They came out of the kitchen and sat on the couch. I knew they were talking about me again. Momma said, "He's been disappearing, Daniel. Hours go by and I don't know where he is."

"What's he say when you ask him where he's been?"

"He tells me he hasn't been anywhere, he says I shouldn't worry. It's so strange, I call him and he's nowhere to be found but a few minutes later he just pops up."

"Doesn't Byron know where he goes?"

"He says he doesn't."

"He *is* being awfully quiet."

"Something's wrong. I wonder if Mr. Robert's friend was right, I wonder if he really did see Kenny in that church afterward. Lord, who knows what that poor baby saw."

"Wilona, he says he only left Grandma Sands's to tell us Joey was O.K. I don't know, what can we do?"

"But Joey swears it was him she followed away from

there, and you know that child would just as soon die as lie. I just wish I knew where he goes. And why."

I had been disappearing, but Momma really didn't need to worry, I wasn't going anywhere. I'd just been going behind the couch for a little while every day. There was a big enough space between the couch and the wall for me to squeeze in back there and just sit in a little ball. It was quiet and dark and still back there.

Byron called this little area the World-Famous Watson Pet Hospital and he made me and Joey believe that magic powers, genies and angels all lived back there. I was waiting to see if that was true.

He started calling it the World-Famous Watson Pet Hospital after we noticed that if something bad happened to one of our dogs or cats they just automatically knew they had to crawl in that space and wait to see if they were going to get better.

Since Momma and Dad had told us that animal doctors cost about a thousand dollars each time you went to them, our pets knew they wouldn't be seeing any veterinarians and that the most help they could get was to crawl behind the couch and see if they could make a deal with the magic powers there.

If one of our dogs got hit by a car and could walk away or if one of them chewed through an electric wire or ran away from home and showed up a couple of weeks later half-starved or something they'd head right for the back of the couch. If one of our cats got beat up by a dog or spent too much time throwing up disgusting pieces of things or got thrown out of a tree or something they'd zip right straight into the World-Famous Watson Pet Hospital.

Those times when one of our pets got hurt I'd wake up the next morning and run out to the living room and climb up on the back of the couch and look over to see how it was doing. If I looked down there and the dog looked up at me with sad eyes and banged his tail a couple of times before he put his head back down, or if the cat looked up and hissed at me, I knew they'd made it through their first night and that the magic powers were probably going to keep them alive. If, when I looked behind the couch, I just saw a crumpled-up yellow towel where the dog or cat had been laying I knew Momma would soon be telling us that Sooty or Fluffy or Scamp or Lady or whoever the patient was hadn't done too well and would be spending the rest of time running around happily in cat or dog heaven. But I knew better. I knew this was some made-up garbage, I knew the magic powers had decided not to keep the animal alive and Dad had got rid of the body before we woke up.

It was kind of strange, because whatever it was that was behind the couch seemed to work best on dogs. Whenever dogs survived the World-Famous Watson Pet Hospital they always came out a lot friendlier. When they came out, they might walk kind of funny but it seemed like all they wanted to do was lick you and wobble around after you wherever you went. Blackie had been in the hospital twice and he got along great with everyone now, even strangers. Even cats.

But cats were different, if one of them survived the hospital it'd come out and give you a dirty look and be a lot meaner than it was before it went in. Most of the time after a cat visited the World-Famous Watson Pet Hospital it wouldn't let anyone but Joetta touch it, but that was O.K., because most of the time nobody but Joetta wanted to touch those stupid cats anyway.

I was waiting to see if the magic powers were going to treat me like a dog or a cat, or if when Byron or Joey woke up one morning they'd find a crumpled-up yellow towel where I was supposed to be.

The only trouble was that the magic powers seemed to be taking a real long time to decide what was going to happen to me. Maybe I wasn't spending enough time back there.

Momma started trying to force me to do more things with Rufus but it seemed like he'd changed while we were gone and wasn't as much fun to be with. Him and Cody got real happy when I gave them my pillowcaseful of dinosaurs. I was getting too mature to play with toys anymore. Momma even forced Byron to take me with him when him and Buphead played basketball, but you didn't have to be Albert Einstein to figure out that the only reason the big guys were playing with me was because Byron had threatened them when my back was turned. But what really bugged me the most was when Momma tried to force me to do things with Joetta.

I'd never noticed what a little crybaby and snitch she was. Every time you turned around she was threatening to go tell on you or was whining about something or being just a plain old pest. After a while to get even with her I wouldn't even look at her. I started hating her guts.

I only wanted to come out of the World-Famous Watson Pet Hospital to eat and go to the bathroom. I even started going into it after Momma and Dad went to bed at night. I started sleeping there.

I spent so much time there that Byron finally figured out where I was going. I looked up one day and there were his eyeballs staring down at me.

"Hi, By."

"Hey, Kenny. So this is where you been hanging out, huh?"

"Are you going to tell on me?"

"Man, when you ever known me to be a snitch?"

"Never."

"You're right." He just kept looking at me. "You want me to get you something to eat?"

"Uh-uh."

Byron walked over and turned on the TV, then stuck his head back behind the couch. "You wanna watch some TV?"

"Uh-uh."

His head disappeared and he watched *Bat Fink*.

When the show was over his head came back. "I'm going to play some ball, you wanna come?"

"I'll come in a minute."

By looked like he didn't believe me. "Cool. Later."

Even though Byron had a reputation for not being a snitch I got the feeling he told on me. When they sat on the couch Momma and Dad quit talking like nobody was around and got real careful about what they said. They started saying stuff about how proud they were of me and what a nice kid I was and junk like that, but it sounded like they'd been practicing what to say. I turned my ears off when they came around. Momma also quit bugging me to find out where I was going. I knew they'd busted me for sure when Joetta's snitchity little face started peeking around the couch every morning.

Byron even started sleeping on the couch at night. Right after Momma and Dad went to bed and I crawled back there he'd come out with his pillow and blanket.

" 'Night, Kenny."

" 'Night, By."

Every morning I'd wake up and Byron would be looking down at me. He'd wake me up by touching the top of my head.

"Hey, Kenny."

"Hi, By."

"You already eat?"

"Uh-uh."

"Come on."

I crawled out from behind the couch and let Byron pour out my cereal and milk. After I finished I said, "Thanks."

"Wait, ain't you gonna change outta them PJs?"

"Oh, yeah."

I changed and went back to the couch. By was sitting there.

"Hold on, Kenny. Watch some cartoons with me."

"O.K., I will in a minute."

Byron grabbed my arm before I could crawl behind the couch. "Naw, man, at least stay for *Felix the Cat*."

"O.K."

I sat next to him on the couch. When Felix was over I thought By would force me to watch more cartoons but he didn't, he let me crawl back behind the couch.

"Check you out later, Kenny."

"See you, By."

As much time as Byron started spending on the couch I thought I was going to have to make room for a bed for him in the World-Famous Watson Pet Hospital. Every time I'd look up he'd be there and we'd have to go eat or watch some TV or go to Mitchell's for something or change clothes or stuff like that.

One day his head popped over the back of the couch and he said, "Come on! I got something to show you!" I knew I had to go, if I wouldn't he'd pull me out by my legs.

I followed Byron upstairs into the bathroom and he stood in front of the sink and looked in the mirror. He scrunched his face up so he could see the bottom of his chin, then he took his thumb and finger and felt around there. He smiled and real slow pulled the thumb and finger away. "Check this out, Jack!"

I looked real close and there was a long, long, skinny black hair growing out of Byron's chin. He held it like it was worth a million dollars.

"And there's another one coming out too!"

198

This made me wonder about my mustache. I hadn't looked at it for a long time and thought it might be pretty long by now.

I climbed up on the toilet and leaned over the sink to see.

Maybe it was because I hadn't looked in the mirror for a long time, but as soon as I saw myself with my lazy eye still being lazy and my face looking so sad I slammed my eyes shut and started crying. I even fell off the toilet. Byron caught me and set me on the floor.

He knew this was some real embarrassing stuff so he closed the bathroom door and sat on the tub and waited for me to stop, but I couldn't. I felt like someone had pulled a plug on me and every tear inside was rushing out, if there was a forest fire somewhere all Smokey the Bear would have to do was hold me upside down over it and the fire wouldn't have a chance.

Byron sat next to me on the floor and put my head in his lap. I still couldn't stop, even though I was soaking him worse than Joey ever drooled on anybody.

It was real embarrassing. "I'm sorry, By."

"Shut up and cry if you want."

That sounded like a real good idea so I did. I think I cried for about two hundred hours.

"Why would they do that, Byron?" I was sounding real bad. My throat was jumping around in my neck and making a bunch of weird noises. "Why would they hurt some little kids like that?"

He waited a long time before he answered, "I don't know, Kenny. Momma and Dad say they can't help themselves, they did it because they're sick, but I don't know. I ain't never heard of no sickness that makes you kill little girls just because you don't want them in your school. I don't think they're sick at all, I think they just let hate eat them up and turn them into monsters. But it's O.K. now, they can't hurt you here. It's all right."

My Adam's apple felt like it was going to blow a hole in my throat but I said, "I did go to the church, By. I saw what happened. I saw two of those little girls. I thought Joey got killed too."

"We all did, Kenny. There ain't nothing wrong with being sad or scared about that. I'm sad about it too. I got real scared too."

"But . . ."

"Man, no one's gonna hurt you here, Kenny."

"But By . . ." I tried to think how to say it. "I'm not scared, I'm just real, real ashamed of myself." That was it. That was the main thing I'd finally found out from being a patient in the World-Famous Watson Pet Hospital.

"Kenny, you ain't got nothing to be ashamed of."

"But you don't know what happened, Byron. You don't know what I did."

"Man, everybody cried. Momma was crying, Dad was scared—he cried too. That was some real scary stuff. That was some real sad stuff."

He still didn't understand. "Byron, I left Joey. I thought the Wool Pooh had her and instead of fighting him like you did, I left, I ran from him. How come you were brave enough to fight him and all I could do was

200

run? All I could save was a shoe, a stupid ripped-up shoe." I couldn't stop crying.

"Awww, man, you ain't gonna start talking that Wool Pooh mess again, are you? I told you the Wool Pooh was some made-up garbage. I told you the only one I was fighting in the water was your stupid little behind, wasn't no one in that water but you and me."

"That's what you think, By, but I know better, I've seen him twice." I couldn't believe Byron was still talking to me. Most of the time if I started sounding weepy and whiny he'd take right off.

"Look, Kenny, if you don't quit talking that Wool Pooh nonsense I'ma leave you in here to cry all alone. There ain't no such thing as a Wool Pooh." Then he stopped sounding so mean and said, "And there ain't no such things as magic powers, neither." I was surprised he'd brought up the magic powers. "You think I don't know why you been hanging out behind the couch?"

He grabbed my ear and twisted my head until I had to look at him. "You think I don't know you waiting for some stupid magic powers or genies or a angel to make you feel better? Dig this: You can wait behind that couch for the rest of your life and ain't no magic powers gonna come back there and make you feel nothing. Only thing that's gonna happen back there is that you gonna stunt your growth from being in a little ball all day." He pulled my ear to make sure I was listening. "If you been spending so much time thinking about how you didn't save Joey why don't you stop and think about why she wasn't in that church, why don't you spend some time thinking about who it was that led her away?"

"But it wasn't me, Byron, I never—"

"Man, shut up and listen." He twisted my ear to make me be quiet.

"Ain't no genies in this world, Kenny, ain't no magic powers, there ain't even no angels, not in this neighborhood anyway. Man, I just don't get you, you supposed to be the one who's so smart. How can you believe in something as stupid as magic powers and genies living behind a couch but not believe it was a part of you that took Joey outta that church?"

Byron started throwing me curveballs. "If you hadn'ta been born who would have took her away from that bomb? No one. If you hadn'ta been born and she walked outta that hot church and saw some stranger waving at her from across the street you think she would have followed him? Ain't no way. She'da gone right back in there. If you hadn't been born who woulda gone in that church to see if Joey really was in there? Me and Momma and Dad was all too scared, you was the only one brave enough to go in there." Every time he made a point he twisted my ear to make me understand better.

"But Byron, it's just not fair. What about those other kids, you know they had brothers and sisters and mommas and daddies who loved them just as much as we love Joey, how come no one came and got them out of that church? How's it fair? How come their relatives couldn't come and warn them?"

202

Byron let go of my ear and thought for a second. "Kenny, things ain't ever going to be fair. How's it fair that two grown men could hate Negroes so much that they'd kill some kids just to stop them from going to school? How's it fair that even though the cops down there might know who did it nothing will probably ever happen to those men? It ain't. But you just gotta understand that that's the way it is and keep on steppin'."

Byron let me sniff and wipe my hand across my eyes before he slid my head back onto the linoleum and stood up. He went over and got some toilet paper and wiped my tears and my boogers off his legs. Then he let a couple of sheets of toilet paper float down and land on me and said, "Blow your nose. Wash your face. You been behind that couch long enough. It's 'bout time you cut this mess out, Momma and Dad beginning to think your little behind is seriously on the blink. Today is the day you check out of the World-Famous Watson Pet Hospital. Don't let me catch you back there no more. You ain't got no cause to be ashamed or scared of nothing. You smart enough to figure this one out yourself. Besides, you getting the word from the top wolf hisself; you gonna be all right, baby bruh. I swear for God."

He walked over to the mirror and scrunched his face up so he could look at his chin again, then used his thumb and finger to pull that long, skinny black hair out a little bit. He let the hair go, smiled at himself and ran his hands along his head like he was brushing his hair. "Shoot," he said, "I sure wish someone would come clean and tell me who my real folks was, there just ain't no way in hell two people as ugly as your momma and daddy could ever have a child as fine as me!"

He blew himself a kiss in the mirror, then left the bathroom. Before he shut the door I could see that Momma and Dad and Joey were standing there in a little knot trying not to let me know they were eavesdropping.

Momma whispered, "What's going on, By? Why was Kenny crying like that, is he O.K.?"

He told her, "Kenny's gonna be cool. He's related to *me*, ain't he?"

"Byron Watson, how many times am I going to have to tell you about saying 'ain't'?"

Some of the time it was hard to figure Byron out. He was very right about some things and he was very wrong about some things. He was very wrong when he said the Wool Pooh was something he'd made up. If he'd ever had his ankle grabbed by it he'd know it was real, if he'd seen the way it was crouched down, crawling around in the dust and the smoke of the church in Birmingham he'd know it wasn't some made-up garbage, if he'd ever seen those horrible toes he'd know the Wool Pooh was as serious as a heart attack.

He was also very wrong about there not being anything like magic powers or genies or angels. Maybe those weren't the things that could make a run-over dog walk without wobbling but they were out there.

Maybe they were in the way your father smiled at you even after you'd messed something up real bad. Maybe they were in the way you understood that your mother wasn't trying to make you the laughing "sock" of the whole school when she'd call you over in front of a bunch of your friends and use spit on her finger to wipe the sleep out of your eyes. Maybe it was magic powers that let you know she was just being Momma. Maybe they were the reason that you really didn't care when the kids would say, "Yuck! You let your momma slob on you?" and you had to say, "Shut up. That's my momma, we got the same germs."

Maybe there were genies in the way your sister would throw a stupid tea party for you and you had fun even though it was kind of embarrassing to sit at a little table and sip water out of plastic teacups.

Maybe there were magic powers hiding in the way your older brother made all the worst thugs in the neighborhood play basketball with you even though you double-dribbled every time they threw you the ball.

And I'm sure there was an angel in Birmingham when Grandma Sands wrapped her little arms around all of the Weird Watsons and said, "My fambly, my beautiful, beautiful fambly."

I climbed up on the toilet and leaned over the sink to take a look. I smiled. Byron was very right about some things too. He was very right when he said I was too smart to believe magic powers lived behind a couch. He also knew what he was talking about when he said I was going to be all right.

Joetta banged on the bathroom door. "Kenny, Byron said you're feeling much better now, if that's right come on out, I gotta go to the bathroom real bad!" She said "real" like it had a million letters in it.

Some of the time I wondered if there really was something wrong with me. A few minutes ago I'd been crying on the floor like a kindergarten baby and now I was looking in the mirror laughing. I blew my nose and splashed a little water on my face 'cause I wanted to go out. Besides, I had to think of a way to get at least half of my dinosaurs back from Rufus.

"Come on in, Joey."

EPILOGUE

At the time of the Watson family's trip, the U.S. South was caught up in a struggle for basic human rights that became known as the civil rights movement. Although the Declaration of Independence states that all men are created equal and the Constitution had been amended after the Civil War to extend the rights and protections of citizenship to African Americans, changing the law of the land did not always change the way people behaved. In the Northern, Eastern and Western states, African Americans often faced discrimination, but it was not as extreme and pervasive as in the South. There communities and states passed laws that allowed discrimination in schooling, housing and job opportunities; prohibited interracial marriages; and enforced segregation by creating separate facilities for African Americans and whites.

In most of the South, African Americans were not permitted to attend the same schools as whites or to use the same parks, playgrounds, swimming pools, hospitals, drinking fountains or bathrooms. Hotels, restaurants and stores would not serve African Americans. The worst sections of public facilities were set aside for "Coloreds Only." White children often attended large, well-equipped, modern schools while African American students went to one-room schoolhouses without enough books or teachers. Rigged laws and "tests" prevented African Americans from voting.

A number of organizations and individuals were working tirelessly to end segregation and discrimination: the National Association for the Advancement of Colored People (NAACP), the Congress of Racial Equality (CORE), and the Southern Christian Leadership Conference (SCLC), as well as Thurgood Marshall, John Lewis, Ralph Abernathy, Medgar Evers, Fannie Lou Hamer and Dr. Martin Luther King, Jr. Along with many other people whose names have been forgotten, these men and women strove to change the laws through nonviolent resistance. They adopted many of the techniques that Mohandas Gandhi had used to liberate India from British rule. Sit-ins and boycotts of stores and public transportation applied economic pressure. Freedom Riders—African Americans and whites—took bus trips throughout the South to test federal laws that banned segregation in interstate transportation. Black students had enrolled in segregated schools such as Central High in Little Rock, Arkansas, and the University of Alabama. Picketing, protest marches, and demonstrations made headlines. Civil rights workers carried out programs for voter education and registration. The goal was to create tension and provoke confrontations that would force the federal government to step in and enforce the laws. Often the tension exploded into gunshots, fires and bombings directed against the people who so bravely fought for change.

The characters and events in this novel are fictional.

However, there were many unsolved bombings in Birmingham at the time of the story, including the one that took place at the Sixteenth Street Baptist Church on September 15, 1963. Four young-teenage girls—Addie Mae Collins, Denise McNair, Carole Robertson and Cynthia Wesley—were killed when a bomb went off during Sunday school. Addie Mae Collins's sister, Sarah, had to have an eye removed, and another girl was blinded. In the unrest that followed the bombing, two other African American children died. Sixteen-year-old Johnny Robinson was shot to death by police, and thirteen-year-old Virgil Wade was murdered by two white boys. Although these may be nothing more than names in a book to you now, you must remember that these children were just as precious to their families as Joetta was to the Watsons or as your brothers and sisters are to you.

Despite the danger, the civil rights movement grew stronger, gaining support all over the country. On August 28, 1963, two hundred thousand people marched on Washington, D.C., to pressure Congress to pass the Civil Rights Bill, and heard Martin Luther King, Jr., deliver his unforgettable "I have a dream" speech. President Lyndon Johnson signed the Civil Rights Bill on July 2, 1964, and signed the Voting Rights Act on August 6, 1965. In 1968 Congress passed the Fair Housing Act.

The individuals who supported the civil rights movement took great risks to force America to change. It was a people's movement, inspired by the courageous acts of ordinary citizens like Rosa Parks, the seamstress from Montgomery, Alabama, who began the first great effort of the movement—the Montgomery bus boycott of 1955–56—when she refused to give up her seat to a white man.

Many heroic people died in the struggle for civil rights. Many others were injured or arrested or lost their homes or businesses. It is almost impossible to imagine the courage of the first African American children who walked into segregated schools or the strength of the parents who permitted them to face the hatred and violence that awaited them. They did it in the name of the movement, in the quest for freedom.

These people are the true American heroes. They are the boys and girls, the women and men who have seen that things are wrong and have not been afraid to ask "Why can't we change this?" They are the people who believe that as long as one person is being treated unfairly, we all are. These are our heroes, and they still walk among us today. One of them may be sitting next to you as you read this, or standing in the next room making your dinner, or waiting for you to come outside and play.

One of them may be you.

Celebrating

CHRISTOPHER PAUL CURTIS

and

The

Watsons

GO TO

BIRMINGHAM

1963

TRIBUTES FROM
Jacqueline Woodson
Kate DiCamillo
Varian Johnson

ORIGINAL MANUSCRIPT PAGES

LETTER FROM THE NEWBERY COMMITTEE

MAP OF THE WATSONS' JOURNEY

NEW AFTERWORD

JACQUELINE WOODSON

Author of *Brown Girl Dreaming* and *Harbor Me*

The first time I read *The Watsons Go to Birmingham—1963,* I was living in a tiny apartment in Brooklyn. It was the 1990s. I lived alone. Very few people knew much about me. And the world had not yet heard of Christopher Paul Curtis, The Author. The book arrived from my editor, Wendy Lamb, who had excitedly found it in, of all places, the slush pile. I remember her letter saying something like "I think there's something here. . . ." I remember reading the first page, thinking I'd just read a paragraph or two and get back to it at another time. Or forget it completely. Back then, not many books came across my desk. Not a whole lot of folks— well, actually No One—was asking for a blurb from me. Wendy was asking me to read it simply to see if I loved it as much as she did. So I read that first page. And then I sat down. I'm sure my mouth was hanging open. I'm sure I screamed. I'm sure I came up out of the Watsons' world, left my apartment, and told the first person I saw (who was probably a stranger) that I'd just read one of the best novels EVER.

The years moved on. I wrote some more books. Found a partner. Gave birth to a baby girl. She turned six, and my partner and I had a son. One year, we read *The Watsons Go to Birmingham—1963* as our Family Read. Then our daughter read it on her own. Then our son. We quoted parts out loud and laughed. We watched the movie (the book is better—just saying!). We bragged about knowing the author.

I imagine my children reading this book with the young people in their own lives one day. And the circle will remain unbroken. And the beauty of *The Watsons Go to Birmingham—1963* will live on.

KATE DiCAMILLO

Author of *Because of Winn-Dixie* and *The Tale of Despereaux*

I was thirty-one years old and working for a book distributor in Minneapolis called the Bookmen. My job title was "picker." This meant that I walked around the third floor of the warehouse and picked books off the shelves and put the books in grocery carts, and then loaded the grocery carts into a creaky freight elevator. I took the elevator to the first floor. I delivered the books to the packing and shipping department, and slowly climbed the stairs back up to the third floor and started all over again.

It was a job that gave me a lot of time to think.

And what I thought about, mostly, was writing.

I was getting up early every morning and writing before I went in to work. I wrote short stories and sent the stories off to literary magazines. In return, the magazines sent me rejection letters, a lot of rejection letters.

But I was happy.

I was finally doing what I had long dreamed of

doing: writing. And I got to spend the day surrounded by books—children's books, mostly, because the third floor of the Bookmen was where the children's books were stocked.

After a while, I started to read some of those children's books. One day, I picked up a novel called *The Watsons Go to Birmingham—1963*.

I thought: "I'll just read the first page."

I was standing in a square of sunlight. My arms were filled with books. My feet hurt. It was late afternoon. I started to read.

And I kept reading.

I laughed out loud.

I kept reading. I laughed out loud again.

I kept reading. I cried.

By the time I got to the end of the book, my whole body was humming. "This," I thought, "this is what I want to try and do—to tell a story that tells the truth, a story that matters, a story that gives the reader hope."

I took a copy of *The Watsons* home with me. I typed up the first chapter to get a feel for how long a chapter in a children's novel would be, how long the entire manuscript would be.

And not long afterward, I started working on a novel about a girl who finds a dog in a grocery store.

Recently, I reread *The Watsons Go to Birmingham—1963*. I laughed aloud again. I cried again. Above all, I was struck by the love in these pages.

"What if the mightiest word is love?" Elizabeth Alexander asks in her poem "Praise Song for the Day."

There's a moment in *The Watsons Go to Birmingham—1963* when the Watsons stop in the Appalachian Mountains on their drive to Alabama. It's very, very dark, but when the family looks up at the sky, they see an impossible number of stars.

"There were more stars in the sky than empty space," says Kenny.

Subtly, gently, this book assures the reader that there is more love in the world than hate, more light than dark—that there are more stars than empty space.

In the end, *The Watsons Go to Birmingham—1963* encourages each of us to do the mightiest thing of all—to love.

This is a book that changes lives.

It certainly changed mine.

VARIAN JOHNSON

Author of *The Parker Inheritance* and *The Great Greene Heist*

Growing up, I hated February.

For sure, part of this dread was because of Valentine's Day. As the son of a florist, I knew that Valentine's Day was the most important business day of the year for us. My father once estimated that 75 percent of our income was centered on that one day.

However, I also knew that my every waking moment outside of school for the week leading up to Valentine's Day would be spent sweeping and mopping floors, de-thorning roses, serving as a human GPS system during deliveries, and trying not to mix up orders from all the neighborhood Casanovas sending flowers to their multiple "lady friends."

Some holiday.

But there was a secondary reason that I disliked February. Every year at the beginning of the month, my school librarian would cart out any and all books featuring black people. After a year of ignoring these books, it was time for Black History Month.

Some might think that, as an avid reader, I would

leap at the opportunity to discover new books featuring people of color. There were certainly plenty of choices—anything from biographies of Rosa Parks, Benjamin Banneker, and of course, Dr. Martin Luther King, Jr., to historical fiction set during American slavery or the civil rights era.

The library was filled with so, so many books about black Americans during February . . . yet I didn't want to read a single title.

It wasn't that the books weren't good. They were enriching. Important. Enlightening. But they were also stifling. Boring. Each book seemed to focus on the struggle—the burden—of being black. What about laughter? Fun? Why couldn't Black History Month also be an opportunity to celebrate black joy, not just the hardship associated with being black?

If only *The Watsons Go to Birmingham—1963* had been available when I was a kid.

The book is as important as any novel set during the civil rights era. When reading the book, we are just as terrorized as the Watsons are on that September day in 1963, when four little girls were killed during the Sixteenth Street Baptist Church bombing. We are just as fearful as Kenny Watson is when sees that small, shiny, shiny black shoe in the rubble—and as he wonders if the shoe belongs to his sister.

But I would argue that the defining moments of the novel aren't about anguish. Rather, they are about joy.

When we first meet the Watsons, they're all sitting on the couch, huddled together, trying to keep warm during the brutal Michigan winter. Then Kenny's dad starts telling stories, and before you know it, all the Watsons are cracking up. They mock each other, but the family's teasing is born of love, not anger or oppression. And we see this love—this joy—throughout the novel as the "weird Watsons" make their way from Flint, Mitch-again, to Alabama and back—all of them packed into the Brown Bomber, Ultra-Glide and all!

The Watsons Go to Birmingham—1963 is a reminder that there is much to celebrate about the black experience: Overcoming oppression. Rising above racism. But perhaps most importantly, the novel reminds us that we can laugh and joke and find joy in ourselves and our families, no matter what the world throws at us.

around a car with the temperature about a million degrees
below zero and each and every one of us crying!

"'top! 'top!" By yelled.

Momma went nuts.   Momma went nuts.

"Daniel Watson, what're we gonna do? "You gotta get this
boy to the hospital! My baby is gonna die!"

Byron didn't need to hear this, he started stamping and
jerking and banging the car door again.

"Daniel, get this boy to the hospital!" Momma's voice
had that "I'm not playing with you" tone and Dad tried to
look serious real quick.

"Wilona, how far do you think I'd get driving down the
street with this little clown attached to the mirror? What am
I supposed to do, have him run beside the car all the way down
to the Emergency Room?"

Momma looked real close at By's mouth, closed her eyes
for a second like she was praying and finally said, "Daniel,
you get in there and call the hospital and see what they say
we should do. Joey and Kenny, go with your daddy.

Dad and Joey went crying into the house. Dad hugged up
to Joey to try to stop her from crying but he was doing it
himself so he was wasting his time. I stayed by the Brown
Bomber. I figured Momma was clearing everybody out for
something. Byron did too and looked at Momma in a real nervous
way.

Momma put her scarf around Byron's face and said,

An original marked manuscript page
during editing with Wendy Lamb

C-19

MOMMA AND JOEY WERE SITTING ON THE COUCH.

"WHAT'S YOUR FATHER DOING?"

"HE'S CUTTING ALL OF BYRON'S HAIR OFF."

MOMMA LAUGHED, JOETTA LOOKED MORE WORRIED THAN EVER.

WE SAT ON THE COUCH FOR A HALF AND HOUR BEFORE DAD AND BY FINALLY CAME DOWNSTAIRS. BY'S ~~PEOPLE~~ NOT ONLY HAD DAD CUT ~~his~~ HAIR OFF HE'D ALSO SHAVED HIS HEAD. BYRON'S HEAD WAS SO SHINY IT LOOKED WET.

POOR BYRON, IF HE'D KNOWN HOW FAR HIS EARS STUCK OUT FROM THE SIDE OF HIS HEAD HE'D NEVER ~~HAVE~~ WOULD HAVE GOTTEN THAT BUTTER.

"WELL, WILONA," DAD SAID, "YOU CAN TELL THIS BOY'S GOT SANDS BLOOD IN HIM, LOOK AT THOSE EARS."

MOMMA LAUGHED, "DON'T BLAME THAT ON MY SIDE OF THE FAMILY, SOMEONE SWITCHED THIS CHILD AT THE HOSPITAL."

I LAUGHED BECAUSE OF BY'S HEAD, JOEY LAUGHED BECAUSE SHE WAS RELIEVED THAT THIS WAS ALL THAT WAS GOING TO HAPPEN TO BY, MOM AND DAD LAUGHED BECAUSE BY LOOKED SO SILLY.

"SO GET THE BROOM AND THE DUSTPAN AND SWEEP THAT GARBAGE UP, THEN STAY IN YOUR ROOM. THIS IS ONLY THE BEGINNING, BYRON. YOU'RE OLD ENOUGH AND YOU'VE BEEN TOLD ENOUGH, SOMETHING'S GOING TO BE DONE THIS TIME." DAD'S FOREHEAD WAS ALL WRINKLED WHEN HE TOLD BYRON THIS.

MOM AND DAD SENT ME AND JO OUTSIDE SO THEY COULD HAVE AN ADULTS ONLY CONFERENCE, ~~AND~~ WHEN JO AND I DRIFTED BACK IN AFTER WHAT WE THOUGHT WAS A GOOD TIME, DAD WAS YELLING INTO THE PHONE.

I DON'T KNOW WHY MY PARENTS THOUGHT YOU HAD TO YELL WHEN MAKING A LONG DISTANCE CALL BUT THEY ALWAYS DID. DAD WAS TALKING TO GRANDMA SANDS, ARRANGING TO DEPORT BYRON OUT OF OUR WORLD.

"O.K, GRANDMA SANDS, WE'LL GET BACK WITH YOU." AND THAT WAS IT, WE HEARD NOTHING ~~MORE~~ ELSE ABOUT SHIPPING BYRON OUT UNTIL ~~THAT DAY~~ A WEEK LATER WHEN DAD BROUGHT THE TT-86-700, ULTRA GLIDE HOME IN THE BROWN BOMBER.

(ESPECIALLY JOEY)

I DON'T KNOW WHY WE DIDN'T CATCH ON THAT SOMETHING WAS REALLY GOING TO HAPPEN THIS TIME, DAD AND MOM BEGAN ACTING STRANGE RIGHT AFTER THAT CALL.

A

MOM STARTED WRITING IN ~~HER~~ NOTEBOOK AND

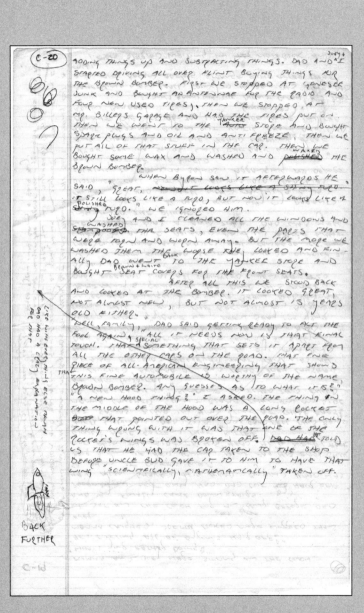

ADDING THINGS UP AND SUBTRACTING THINGS. DAD AND I
STARTED DRIVING ALL OVER FLINT BUYING THINGS FOR
THE BROWN BOMBER. FIRST WE STOPPED AT GENESEE
JUNK AND BOUGHT AN ANTENNAE FOR THE RADIO AND
FOUR NEW USED TIRES, THEN WE STOPPED AT
MR. BILLEYS GARAGE AND HAD THE TIRES PUT ON.
THEN WE WENT TO THE YANKEE STORE AND BOUGHT
SPARK PLUGS AND OIL AND ANTI FREEZE, THEN WE
PUT ALL OF THAT STUFF IN THE CAR. THEN WE
BOUGHT SOME WAX AND WASHED AND WAXED THE
BROWN BOMBER.

WHEN BYRON SAW IT AFTERWARDS HE
SAID, "GREAT, NOW IT LOOKS LIKE A SHINY TURD.
IT STILL LOOKS LIKE A TURD, BUT NOW IT LOOKS LIKE A
SHINY POLISHED TURD." WE IGNORED HIM.

JOEY AND I CLEANED ALL THE WINDOWS AND
WASHED THE SEATS, EVEN THE PARTS THAT
WERE TORN AND WORN AWAY. BUT THE MORE WE
WASHED THEM THE WORSE THE SEATS LOOKED AND FIN-
ALLY DAD WENT BACK TO THE YANKEE STORE AND
BOUGHT BROWN + WHITE SEAT COVERS FOR THE FRONT SEATS.

AFTER ALL THIS WE STOOD BACK
AND LOOKED AT THE BOMBER. IT LOOKED GREAT,
NOT ALMOST NEW, BUT NOT ALMOST 15 YEARS
OLD EITHER."

"WELL, FAMILY," DAD SAID GETTING READY TO ACT THE
FOOL AGAIN, "ALL IT NEEDS NOW IS THAT FINAL
SPECIAL TOUCH. THAT SOMETHING THAT SETS IT APART FROM
ALL THE OTHER CARS ON THE ROAD. THAT ONE
PIECE OF ALL-AMERICAN ENGINEERING THAT SHOWS
THAT THIS FINE AUTOMOBILE IS WORTHY OF THE NAME
BROWN BOMBER. ANY GUESSES AS TO WHAT IT IS?"
"A NEW HOOD THING?" I ASKED. THE THING IN
THE MIDDLE OF THE HOOD WAS A LONG ROCKET
BOMB THAT POINTED OUT OVER THE ROAD. THE ONLY
THING WRONG WITH IT WAS THAT ONE OF THE
ROCKET'S WINGS WAS BROKEN OFF. DAD HAD TOLD
US THAT HE HAD THE CAR TAKEN TO THE SHOP
BEFORE UNCLE BUD GAVE IT TO HIM TO HAVE THAT
WING "SCIENTIFICALLY, MATHEMATICALLY" TAKEN OFF.

BACK
FURTHER

AMERICAN LIBRARY ASSOCIATION
ASSOCIATION FOR LIBRARY
SERVICE TO CHILDREN

50 EAST HURON STREET CHICAGO, ILLINOIS 60611-2795 U.S.A.
312-280-2163   800-545-2433, EXT. 2163
FAX: 312-280-3257

Christopher Paul Curtis   January 31, 1996
2439 Rossini Blvd.
Windsor, Ontario
Canada N8W-4P9

Dear Chris:

On behalf of the 1996 John Newbery Committee please accept our congratulations on
winning a Newbery Honor Book for <u>The Watsons Go To Birmingham-1963</u> (Delacorte).

The Committee tried valiantly to reach you on the morning of January 22. We were all
very excited when your wife told us you were at work on another manuscript in the
Children's Room at the Windsor Public Library. After several days of intense
discussion it is a thrill to call the winners and hear their reaction.

You should know that this is the 75th anniversary of the Newbery Medal. The
Association for Library Service to Children (ALSC) is planning a year of special
recognition for the award beginning with the ALA Annual Conference in New York.

We look forward to seeing you this summer and sharing in the festivities for all the
award winners.

My Best,

Mary Beth Dunhouse

Mary Beth Dunhouse
Chair, 1996 Newbery Award Committee

Letter from the Newbery Committee

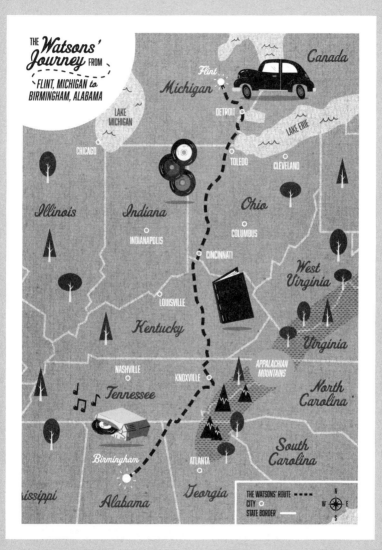

THE *Watsons' Journey* FROM ~FLINT, MICHIGAN to~ BIRMINGHAM, ALABAMA

Canada

Flint

Michigan

LAKE MICHIGAN

DETROIT

LAKE ERIE

CHICAGO

TOLEDO

CLEVELAND

Illinois

Indiana

Ohio

COLUMBUS

INDIANAPOLIS

CINCINNATI

West Virginia

LOUISVILLE

Kentucky

Virginia

NASHVILLE

KNOXVILLE

APPALACHIAN MOUNTAINS

North Carolina

Tennessee

Birmingham

ATLANTA

South Carolina

ississippi

Alabama

Georgia

THE WATSONS' ROUTE ----
CITY ○
STATE BORDER —

N
W ✦ E
S

AFTERWORD

I'm often asked, "If you could go back and change anything in one of your books, what would it be?"

I answer by turning into Captain Pompous. I intone, "Nothing. I wouldn't change one comma. A novel is much like a snapshot of a particular time, and part of the snapshot is the photographer's or author's frame of mind at the moment the picture was taken. I believe that is something that must be respected."

Another reason I'm opposed to changing what I've written is I'd have to reread the book to do so, something I avoid. I know rereading means I'll be tormented by words and phrases that should be changed. I'm also sure to be assaulted by whole stretches that should be eliminated, and there's always a character who should have been bumped off much earlier.

I look upon rereading as a Sisyphean task, an exercise in futility, because even though there is a last page to a novel, the truth is the story is never over. If allowed, I would go on and on adding and subtracting from my work. The most difficult part of writing for me is knowing when to end the story.

Therefore the flaws, quirks, and scars of the original book should be left alone.

I bought that nonsense until sometime in the early 2000s. I was presenting to an auditorium of fifth graders and, after speaking, was asked to read something from *The Watsons Go to Birmingham—1963*. My go-to chapter in such cases is the opening one, where Byron gets his lips stuck to a frozen mirror.

I read, *"It was one of those super-duper-cold Saturdays. One of those days that when you breathed out your breath . . ."*

A student's flailing arm distracted me.

Most times I would have ignored her—I've found that these overly enthusiastic "Ooh, ooh, ooh!" question askers tend to wear themselves out quickly. But this girl had been attentive and interested throughout my talk. It was painfully obvious that she loved reading and books. Teachers and visiting authors can spot this type of child a mile off; they might as well have a scarlet *B* for *bookworm* tattooed on their foreheads. I love and identify with them—this girl was one of *my* people—so I stopped reading and said, "If you have any questions I'll answer them at the end of the chapter. I promise you'll be first."

She said, "I don't have a question, Mr. Curtis,

but could you please, please, please read chapter six instead?"

Good for you, I thought. If you want something, the first step is having the courage to ask for it!

"Sure," I said, "I'll read chapter six. Why not?"

I turned to page 75 and began reading.

Never having read this chapter aloud, I found myself fumbling through it with a host of "uhs," "ums," and "just a seconds." When I looked up to apologize for the subpar reading, the fifth graders' heads were bobbing in encouragement and their widened eyes were locked on me. I kid you not, many of the little darlings were leaning forward, actually sitting on the edges of their seats.

Wow! I told myself. This is going better than I thought. I'm knocking this baby right out of the park!

I continued reading chapter six.

It wasn't until I was on page eighty-two, right before "The Word," that I realized this pack of ten-year-old clowns had set me up.

And the ringleader was little Miss Bookworm.

I read, *"Finally I said, 'So, By, how about you and me doing a little cussing?'*

"He twisted up his face and said, 'I thought I told your jive little . . .'"

I froze.

I looked up. Their eyes were still locked on me.

I looked at the teacher, who shrugged and gave me an "Oh, well" smirk.

I went back to the book: yup, there it was, the rare three-lettered word that starts with *a*.

My lips opened and shut soundlessly.

I couldn't do it. I couldn't read the word aloud to these fifth graders.

My eyes went to Miss Bookworm, who had sprung the trap.

"It's okay," she encouraged me. "Go ahead and read it. We already know what the word is."

My thought process in situations like this is similar to the way I used to play basketball—eventually effective but painfully slow and plodding. It seemed I stood in front of that class for hours, trying to figure what to do.

I thought back to the many times when I'd take questions after a talk and some child would ask, "Why did you use swear words in this book?"

My stock response has always been "Are there any words in there that you don't hear at school every day? I'm sure you heard much worse on the way into the auditorium today, right? That's been the language of the playground for so long that Bam-Bam and Pebbles used to speak that way."

Then Captain Pompous would ride again and I'd look down from astride my horse and say, "One of the things I do as an author is strive for authenticity."

Finally I'd go politician on the questioner. I'd point at someone else and say, "Next question, please."

But as I stood in front of those fifth graders sometime in the early 2000s, my thoughts went to the teachers I've put in the same situation, one where they have to decide how to handle the few examples of profanity in *The Watsons*. I felt that what I had done was both unnecessary and unfair. As I stammered in front of those kids, I remember thinking, Man, if I could go back and rewrite this I'd do it in a heartbeat.

We jump ahead to 2017 and a call from Wendy Lamb. She began telling me about plans for the twenty-fifth-anniversary edition of *The Watsons Go to Birmingham—1963.*

It's not often that life doles out second chances, and I knew this was my opportunity.

So, after much thought and consideration, I made some minor changes in this new edition.

If you have read an earlier edition of *The Watsons* and read this one now, I hope you didn't even notice.

Self-bowdlerization?

No. More a realization that there is more than one way to skin a cat. In *Hocus Pocus* Kurt Vonnegut wrote, "Profanity and obscenity entitle people who don't want unpleasant information to close their eyes and ears to you." Over the past twenty-five years I've had and read discussions where the few "bad words" in *The Watsons* are used as an excuse to in effect ban the book and stamp "Unsuitable for young readers" on it.

I don't want that.

Walter Dean Myers is also partially responsible for these changes. Soon after the publication of the book we had a great conversation about writing. The gist of what he told me was that writers, particularly African American writers, have a responsibility to get our books into the hands of as many children as we possibly can, that if we provide accurate, interesting reflections of their lives it will serve as a nudge to get them into reading. And if they can master reading their lives will be markedly better.

Walter's words had an immediate impact on the way I write. I became much more conscientious about how young people receive what I've written; I want more youngsters to read my books, to smile and nod in recognition; I want the book to be something that lets them know, "You're not the only one who has felt this way. Others of us have gone through the same things."

And if changing a few words in *The Watsons Go to Birmingham—1963* will get this book and others into more children's hands, good old Captain Pompous will have to find some other way to be authentic.

ACKNOWLEDGMENTS

If I were to list all of the people who contributed to the making of *The Watsons Go to Birmingham—1963,* we'd need forty more pages. Here are a but a few.

I'd like to thank the many teachers, librarians, administrators, professors, and parents who have made this book accessible to so many young people, particularly: Leslie Acevedo, Roland Alums, Robert Bennet, Pauletta Bracy, Ellen Brothers, Angela Brown, Janet Brown, Jean Brown, Lois Buckman, Rose Casement, Margarite Davidson, Terry Fisher, Gail Ganakas, Victor Greene, Len Hayward, Roz Ivey, Suzanne Henry Jakeway, John Jarvey, Colleen Kammer, Ron Karr, Harriet Kenworthy, Don Lada, Teri Lesesne, Cary Loren, Wendy Nancoo, John Nash, John Rhymes, Richard Russell, Elaine Stephenson, Don Stewart, Deb Taylor, and Traki Taylor.

A ton of thanks and admiration to the many people in my family at Delacorte and Random House who polished and presented my baby: John Adamo, Terry Borzumato, Dana Carey, Melanie Chang, Katrina Damkoehler, Cletus Durkin, Colleen Fellingham, Judith Haut, Beverly Horowitz,

Alison Kolani, Gillian Levinson, Barbara Perris, Tamar Schwartz, Andrew Smith, Craig Virden, Adrienne Waintraub and her amazing School and Library team, and Sales, Publicity, and Marketing. And most especially to the magnificent Wendy Lamb. Even more important than finding a great editor twenty-five years ago, I was fortunate enough to discover a great friend.

And to the many authors I've gotten to know, thank you for your support, kind words, and friendship. (We have chosen such a great profession chock full of wonderful people haven't we?): Elizabeth Acevedo, Kwame Alexander, Laurie Halse Anderson, Ashley Bryan, Floyd Cooper, Robert Cormier, Chris Crutcher, Kate DiCamillo, Varian Johnson, David Barclay Moore, Walter Dean Myers, Jason Reynolds, Jerry Spinelli, Vince Vawter, Rita Williams-Garcia, Jackie Woodson, and Michele Landsberg of Toronto.

And to my fellow Flintstones, a million thanks for your encouragement and support: Alvin Ricky Banks, Ricardo Brandon, Roy Breed, Billy Calloway, Jeff Dominguez, Jenni Dones, Phil Gonzales, Wade Jackson, Julie Jones, John Love, Steve Mariotti, Ernie Nelson, Chester Stockard, Michel Taylor, Douglas Tennant, Liz Ivette Torres, Henri Watkins, Jimmy Wesley, and Henry Younger.

To my family, Leslie Jane Curtis, Herman Elmer Curtis Jr, Herman David Curtis, Lindsey Curtis, Cydney Curtis, Sarah Curtis, and Michael Curtis, I can never thank you enough, big love to all!

And finally to the ones who deal with me every day, the Curtii: Habon, Ayaan, Ebyaan, and Libaan, you are my greatest happiness, thank you, thank you, thank you!

CHRISTOPHER PAUL CURTIS won the Newbery Medal and the Coretta Scott King Award for his bestselling second novel, *Bud, Not Buddy*. His first novel, *The Watsons Go to Birmingham—1963,* was also singled out for many awards, and has been a bestseller in hardcover and paperback. His most recent novels for Random House include *The Mighty Miss Malone, Mr. Chickee's Messy Mission, Mr. Chickee's Funny Money,* and *Bucking the Sarge.*

Christopher Paul Curtis grew up in Flint, Michigan. After high school he began working on the assembly line at the Fisher Body Plant No. 1 while attending the Flint branch of the University of Michigan. He is now a full-time writer, and lives with his family in Windsor, Ontario.

nobodybutcurtis.com